'Everyone falls in love.

Whether you're in love with the boy
next door or somebody in your French class,
it makes no difference to how you feel.
Dare you speak to the object of your affection?
What will they say?
Maybe it's better not to risk it!
But then you'll always wonder . . . what if?

Sweet Hearts are for those of you who love,
have loved and will love. So, in a way, they're
for everyone . . . everywhere . . . for ever.
Happy dreams ever after!'

Look out for more

SWEET HEARTS: DEEP WATER
A RED FOX BOOK 978 1 849 41219 3

First published in Great Britain by Red Fox Books,
an imprint of Random House Children's Publishers UK,
A Random House Group Company

This edition published 2012

1 3 5 7 9 10 8 6 4 2

The Random House Group Limited supports The Forest Stewardship Council
(FSC®), the leading international forest certification organization. Our books
carrying the FSC label are printed on FSC®-certified paper. FSC is the only forest
certification scheme endorsed by the leading environmental organizations,
including Greenpeace. Our paper procurement policy can be found
at www.randomhouse.co.uk/environment

MIX
Paper from
responsible sources
FSC® C016897

Set in Birka 12/15.5pt by Falcon Graphic Art Ltd

Random House Children's Publishers UK,
61–63 Uxbridge Road, London W5 5SA

www.kidsatrandomhouse.co.uk
www.totallyrandombooks.co.uk
www.randomhouse.co.uk

Addresses for companies within The Random House Group Limited
can be found at: www.randomhouse.co.uk/offices.htm

THE RANDOM HOUSE GROUP Limited Reg. No. 954009

A CIP catalogue record for this book is available from the British Library.

Printed and bound in Great Britain by CPI Group (UK) Ltd, Croydon. CR0 4YY

For Phil, my very own sweetheart

*and for Jemima, who brings a smile
to my face every day*

*With grateful thanks to Adele Carlsen,
Katie Clark and the members of
the British Synchronized Swimming Team*

Deep Water

Chapter 1

a golden ticket

The sounds were muffled, the voice distorted, and the light shimmered and flickered, changing every second. Pearl held herself perfectly straight under the water for a moment, her legs stretching to the ceiling, her toes pointed. Then she swiftly drew her arms across her body, pulling herself downwards in a spiral. One . . . two turns, and she knew by instinct that her toes had vanished under the water. Quickly, she drew in her knees and turned herself round. Her head burst through the surface at exactly the same time as the seven other girls, and each of them wore a bright smile.

'Good,' said the woman watching from the side, putting down her microphone. She had short blonde hair that curled naturally, and it was her voice that Pearl had heard coming through the underwater speakers of the three-metre-deep pool. Bonnie Rose had been the team's coach for two years, and she was strict but fair. All the girls liked her. 'I think that's enough for now.'

The eight girls swam to the side, where they were joined by four others who had watched the routine but not taken part. Pearl felt a quiver of nerves. She wasn't quite sure how she'd got through the routine without making any mistakes. All the girls were on edge this morning because today they would be told which of them had made the final selection for the Olympics. There were only eight places, with one reserve, but there were currently twelve girls in the British synchro team – which meant that three of them wouldn't be going at all, and another would probably have to watch the whole competition from the sidelines . . .

Pearl hoped fervently that she would make the team, but then she knew they all felt the same way. And she was the youngest too – what if Bonnie and Emily, the team manager, decided she was too young this time? The disappointment would be awful.

Bonnie crouched down on the tiles by the pool. 'Thanks, everyone, for your hard work this morning. I know it hasn't been easy but we'll put you out of your misery after lunch. Meet us in reception at two o'clock and we'll let you know our final line-up for the team.'

Pearl hauled herself out of the pool alongside her best friend, Millie, whose blue eyes looked anxious. Millie caught her glance and pulled a funny face. Pearl knew what she was thinking. *Have we done enough? Were we good enough to get one of those places?*

It was like a golden ticket. The Olympics in London! There wouldn't be another opportunity like this – ever. And suddenly Pearl was absolutely sure she hadn't made it. Three girls would be dropped from the team, and she just knew one of them would be her. Perhaps it would be better to be dropped altogether than to get the reserve place? To do all the training and then not actually swim – that would be worse than not getting your hopes up at all, wouldn't it?

Pearl felt her eyes fill with tears. What would she tell her dad, who had spent years faithfully ferrying her to and from training sessions and sitting through tests and competitions?

The chatter in the changing room was quieter than usual. Even Jen Sugden, the oldest and most experienced in the team at twenty-seven, seemed preoccupied, and snapped at Pearl as she accidentally knocked her clothes onto the floor. 'Watch what you're doing!'

'Sorry,' Pearl apologized quickly. She wiped her eyes, hoping no one would notice that she was trying not to cry.

'I can't eat,' Millie said as they sat down in the cafeteria. It was a big, airy room, with windows all along one side. At the moment, there were only a few other people sitting at the tables, two of them with laptops open. The centre was open to the public at weekends, but during the week it was used by professional athletes and private sports groups, so it tended to be a quiet, highly-focused place. Millie stared at her sandwich. 'I can't possibly eat; I'll be sick.'

'You've got to eat something,' Pearl told her. 'You'll never be able to swim this afternoon if you don't get some calories into you.'

The girls burned twice as many calories as a non-athlete every day, so it was important to eat regularly. But Pearl didn't feel hungry either. 'Who do you think will make it?' she asked in a whisper, glancing around to make sure none of the other girls was within earshot.

Millie leaned forward. They'd had this conversation hundreds of times before. 'Well, based on this morning's session, I'd say Sandra could be in trouble. Did you see how she winced after we'd done the lift section? If she's not strong enough to be base any more . . .'

Both of them turned to look over at Sandra, a tall girl with long brown hair, who was sitting on her own at a table by the window. 'She looks worried,' said Pearl, but at that moment Sandra glanced round, and both of them immediately swung back to their food, guilty.

'I hate this,' Millie said, staring at her sports bottle.

'You have to eat, Mills.'

'No, I mean, I hate all *this* – staring at each other, wondering who's got in and wishing bad things on other people.'

Pearl's eyes widened. 'Wishing bad things . . . ?'

Millie flapped her hands in distress. 'Oh no, no, I didn't mean that. You know what I mean – we all want a place. And some people won't get one. Don't you honestly, in your heart of hearts, have a tiny hope that someone else will get an injury or something? So that you'll be in for sure?'

Pearl opened her mouth and then shut it again.

'There – see?' said Millie. 'It doesn't make us bad people, does it?'

'What doesn't?' asked Evie, coming to join her friends. Evie was the shortest member of the team, with thick blonde hair and a round smiley face. She was a couple of years older than Millie and Pearl, but the three of them had bonded during a training camp last summer and were now inseparable.

'Do you wish for the other girls to have accidents so you can get a place on the team?' asked Pearl in a low voice.

'All the time,' said Evie cheerfully. 'Doesn't every-one?'

Pearl bit her lip. 'It's horrible.'

'We're competitors,' Evie told her. 'It's natural to think like that. But it's not like I'd trip them up on the way to the lockers, or give anyone food poisoning. It's just that, if someone *happened* to pull a muscle, which goes on all the time in practices, let's face it – well . . .' She shrugged expressively. 'Let's just say I'd be buying them a big bunch of flowers while trying on my official Team GB strip.'

The other two laughed. 'You're awful,' said Millie, half admiringly. 'I don't know how you can say stuff like that.'

'It's only what everyone's thinking,' said Evie. 'I don't see the point of pretending otherwise.'

Pearl smiled at Millie. Evie was easily the most outspoken of the three, though Pearl suspected that sometimes she did it just to show off. As the youngest

6

swimmers, they looked up to people like Jen, and to Kat and Lizzie, the twins, who were always getting into trouble for speaking out of turn. Pearl loved all the girls like sisters but she felt like the baby most of the time, especially when they went out as a group and it was very obvious who had reached the magic age of eighteen and who hadn't.

'What are you going to do if you're not chosen?' Millie asked Evie.

'Take up sky-diving,' said Evie promptly. 'No, honestly! I mean, it's all about the Olympics, isn't it? If I don't make it . . . well, I'm not sure I want to do it any more.'

'Bonnie would say that's a defeatist attitude,' Pearl teased her.

'I don't care,' said Evie. 'I want to be the best – part of the best team in the country. And if I can't be that, then I don't think I want to try. You know what I mean?'

Pearl wasn't sure she did. She didn't feel that way about swimming. If she wasn't picked for the team, she'd be devastated, but she couldn't imagine giving it up altogether. She'd keep trying, wouldn't she? Surely nothing else could be as amazing as swimming? Nothing would stop her carrying on – nothing but an injury, that is. Her heart plummeted. That would be the worst thing in the world, not to be able to swim any more.

Millie waved a hand in front of her friend's face. 'Earth to Pearl, hello?'

Pearl smiled. 'Sorry.'

'We're all thinking about this far too much,' declared Evie. 'What will be will be and all that. We should talk about something completely different.'

'Like what?' asked Pearl.

Evie paused. 'Er . . .'

There was silence. Pearl sighed and looked at her watch. Twelve forty-five. It was going to be a long lunch break.

♥

You could have heard a pin drop as the girls stared expectantly at their team manager, Emily Van Hest. Beside her stood Bonnie. Twelve anxious faces looked up at them; at the two people who could make or break their dreams.

'We won't keep you in suspense,' Emily said, looking from one girl to the next. 'But we do want to thank you all for your continued hard work and dedication, and for putting in the extra hours recently. We have taken everything into consideration – not just your performance in recent weeks but also your medical histories and your teamwork skills.'

Pearl reached for Millie's hand and squeezed it. Millie gripped it back, her eyes still fixed firmly on Emily.

'To those of you who haven't made it this time,' went on Emily, 'we are very, very sorry. And although you'll no longer be training with us, we will make every effort to place you in high-performance club squads so that you can continue your careers. Of course, it goes without saying that once the Games are over, we'll bring you all back here to continue training for the Worlds and the Europeans.' She took a piece of paper from the table. 'Right, this is the final list. The following eight girls will be competing in the London 2012 Olympics.'

Pearl closed her eyes. Her heart was thumping so loudly, she was sure everyone in the room could hear it. Her head felt dizzy.

Emily began reading. 'Elizabeth Benson-Rowe, Katherine Benson-Rowe . . .'

The twenty-year-old twins grinned at each other in relief.

'Primrose Cayley, Georgie Harrison, Evelyn Ivory . . .'

Millie's grip tightened. Her surname was Edwards, which meant, if Emily was reading alphabetically, that Millie wasn't on the list . . .

'Pearl Okeke . . .'

Pearl's breath felt as if it had been sucked out of her body. It was a good thing she was sitting down, she realized, because her knees would have given way. She had made it! She was going to the Olympics!

Emily was continuing. 'Jennifer Sugden, Hollie-Mae Webb. And the team reserve will be Millie Edwards.' She looked up. 'That's it. Congratulations to those of you who've made it, commiserations to those who haven't. Bonnie and I will be on hand for the next half an hour in our offices if any of you want to come to talk to us. And Steve is expecting you in the gym at two-thirty.' She gave a smile. 'It's going to be a very exciting year.'

As Emily and Bonnie left the room, there was an outburst of noise. The twins hugged each other and anyone else they could reach. Jen sat there, stunned, repeating, 'I thought they'd say I was too old. I honestly never thought I'd make it . . .' And Hollie-Mae burst into happy tears.

Sprinkled between the joyous ones were the girls sitting with white faces and tears springing to their eyes. Pearl saw Sandra Cousins, the girl they'd been discussing at lunch time, get up abruptly and leave the room, her hands over her face. Evie's words came back to her: *I'd be buying them a big bunch of flowers while trying on my official Team GB strip*. She wondered if Evie felt like that now. All this passed through her head in a flash before Evie swept her off her chair into an enormous hug. 'We made it!' she sang. 'We did it!'

Millie was quiet, trying to smile but not quite managing it. 'You're coming with us, Mills!' cried Evie. 'We're all going!'

'Yeah,' said Millie, but her voice wobbled. 'I guess.'

'Reserve's not so bad,' said Pearl, hoping she sounded convincing. 'You know what it's like — one of us is bound to be injured or ill or something . . .'

Her friend stood up, pulling away from Pearl's outstretched hand. 'I don't want to swim if one of you is injured. I don't want to get onto the team if someone else is ill. I want to be on the team because I'm *good enough to be there* . . .' Tears suddenly streamed down her face and she turned and ran out of the room.

Pearl and Evie stared at each other in dismay. Pearl wanted to feel overjoyed — she'd made it, she was going to be competing at the Olympics! But her best friend was only the reserve, and that took the shine off the great news.

'She'll come round,' Evie said. 'I'm sure she'll be fine.'

'Maybe we should go after her.' Pearl rose to her feet, but Evie pulled her back down.

'Not right now. Give her a few minutes. We're probably not the people she wants to see.' Evie grinned. 'Besides, we need a minute to ourselves. You made it, Pearl! The youngest on the team! Aren't you manic with delight?'

Pearl's face broke into a smile. 'Of course I am. It's like – the best present you could ever have. I can't really believe it.'

'I can't wait to tell my mum,' said Evie. 'She's been preparing me for the worst all week.'

'I want to tell my dad first,' said Pearl. 'He's the one who kept me going, who came to all my competitions. He's the one who took me swimming when I was a baby.'

'He's going to be so proud of you. You should ring him right now,' Evie told her.

'No,' Pearl disagreed. 'I want to wait to tell him face to face.'

'You're going to hang on until you get home?' Evie stared in disbelief. 'We've got the whole afternoon to get through! You mean you're not going to ring anyone to tell them?'

'No,' said Pearl firmly. 'I want to wait till I can see my dad and tell him in person. He should be the first one to know, and I want to see his expression when I tell him.' Her face lit up. 'It's going to be *brilliant*.'

Chapter 2

you could probably snap me in half

Pearl had gradually got used to the tough training hours, missing her school friends and collapsing into bed every night. But six months later, she still hadn't got used to the interviews. There weren't very many, usually – synchronized swimming wasn't as high-profile a sport as many others – but every now and then, she would be asked to say a few words for a website or a magazine article.

Today, she, Millie and Evie, as the youngest members of the team, had all been asked to give an interview for the Parchester *Youth Voice* magazine in a small meeting room. It meant they were missing part of their lunch break, but with two hours to fill every day, they were quite pleased to have something different to do.

As they went into the room, Pearl was conscious of a feeling of surprise. The interviewer was already there – a boy not much older than herself. He got up immediately, smiling. 'Hiya, I'm Bailey Ross. Thanks for coming to talk to me.'

They all shook hands with him while he checked their names. 'You're a bit younger than our usual interviewers,' Evie told him, sounding amused.

Bailey nodded. 'I know. I won a competition to be the new reporter on the magazine.' He said it simply, without any hint of arrogance. 'This is my second article for them.'

'Congratulations.' Pearl was impressed. He seemed very confident for his age, with dark skin, even darker than hers, and deep brown eyes set in a round, friendly face.

'Thanks.' He put a small recording device on the table. 'I hope it's OK – I'm going to record our conversation so that I don't have to take notes while we talk.'

The girls nodded. They were familiar with this. In fact, shortly after the team was selected, they'd all been to a talk by a media consultant, who gave them lots of advice about how much to reveal on social networking sites and how to handle interviews. 'Don't talk too fast,' she had said, 'and don't be afraid of silences. Think before you speak, but try to be natural.' Pearl had exchanged puzzled glances with her friends.

How could they be 'natural' and yet 'speak slowly'? She'd done several interviews now but she still wasn't sure she'd cracked it.

Bailey switched on the recorder and made sure the little red light was on. 'OK,' he said, 'I'm just going to fire questions at you all, if you don't mind.'

'That's fine,' replied Evie.

'I want to ask each of you how it feels to be selected for the Olympic synchro team,' Bailey said. 'Evelyn?'

Evie took a deep breath. 'Amazing,' she said. 'It's like Christmas and birthday all at once. But also there's so much pressure. We're representing our country – that's a big thing and we don't want to let anyone down. I want to make my family and friends proud of me.'

Bailey smiled. 'Thanks. Millie, what about you?'

Millie hesitated. 'I'm the team reserve, which means I do all the training that the other girls do, but I probably won't get to swim at the competition.'

'That must be hard,' suggested Bailey.

Millie nodded. 'It was to start with. I was upset that I'd got so close but not close enough. But now I try not to think about it at all. Besides, we have so much training to do, you have to stay focused on improving performance. It's a great honour, obviously, and we're all really excited.'

Bailey turned to Pearl. 'What about you, Pearl? You're the youngest in the team, aren't you?'

'Yes.' Pearl stopped. Her mind was a blank. Evie and Millie had said it all, hadn't they? What could she add? 'I agree with the others,' she said lamely.

There was sympathy in Bailey's eyes, as though he realized she couldn't think of anything to say. 'What about your family and friends? What did they say when you told them you'd been picked?'

'Oh.' Pearl's mind flashed back to that day – that brilliant, awful day. Getting a lift with Millie's mum and running to her front door, flinging it open and calling for Dad – who wasn't there. Being met by Mum, whose eyes were red with crying, who could hardly speak for sobs. The day her Olympic dream had come true and her dad had walked out. Dreams made and broken all at once. What could she say? 'Um – well, they were really pleased, of course.'

'Everyone at school said you were a celebrity, didn't they?' prompted Millie.

Pearl felt grateful to her friend. Millie had helped her through that terrible time; she knew all about the break-up and she'd guessed that Pearl wouldn't be able to answer easily. 'Yes, they did. They went all stupid about it and started bowing and curtseying every time they saw me. And pretending to take photos.'

'Did that annoy you?' asked Bailey.

'No, no. No, it was funny.' Pearl smiled, and Bailey smiled back. For a moment he paused, as though he'd forgotten what he was going to say next. Then he blinked and said, 'But you don't go to school any more, is that right? You and Millie?'

'Yeah,' said Millie. 'British swimming laws say if you're picked you can't attend school in the year leading up to the Olympics. To be honest, it wouldn't really be possible anyway, not with the amount of training we do.'

'Do you miss your friends?' asked Bailey, his eyes still on Pearl.

She thought for a moment. 'Yes – yes, I guess so. Sometimes. Sometimes they tell me they've been out at a gig or a party or something and I feel sad that I wasn't there. They used to ask me along to start with, but I could hardly ever go, and so they stopped asking.'

'That must be difficult.'

'Yes – no. It does bother me occasionally, but I have such good friends on the team . . .' She smiled at Millie and Evie. 'We spend so much time together, we're all like sisters. And I do sometimes catch up with my school friends, but it's hard when we're all so busy doing stuff.'

'You said there was a lot of training,' commented Bailey. 'What sort of hours do you do?'

'We train every day from seven thirty a.m. to five in the afternoon,' Evie told him. 'With a two-hour lunch break. That's Monday to Friday. We train for three hours on Saturdays too, in the morning.'

Bailey's gaze swung round to her and his jaw dropped. 'But that's— *Really?* That much time?'

The three girls nodded. 'People think synchro is an easy sport,' said Evie, her tone hardening slightly. 'But it isn't. We're as fit as any other athlete competing at the Games – fitter in some ways than most of the others.'

'Can you give me an example?' asked Bailey. 'I mean, what sort of things do you have to do?'

The girls exchanged glances. 'Um – well, we have to spend a lot of time underwater,' said Millie. 'So we do a lot of lengths underwater. We can all swim two lengths of the pool without coming up for air.'

Bailey's eyebrows shot up. 'Two lengths? Wow.'

'And there's a core endurance machine in the gym,' added Evie. 'You have to do thirty seconds of high-impact, high-stress activity before you switch to another activity. You keep going for as long as you can. Our strength and conditioning coach, Steve Cole, can do four and a half minutes.'

'What about you?' asked Bailey.

Evie grinned. 'We can all do over seven minutes. Some of us can do eight.'

Bailey let out his breath slowly. 'So you guys are actually fitter than your coach?'

'Kind of.'

'Wow.' He seemed lost for words again. 'So how do you feel when people say that synchro is an easy sport – or not even a sport at all?'

'It's not really fair,' said Evie, with a frown. 'They don't usually know anything about it.'

'Yeah,' agreed Millie. 'It's a bit like people saying footballers are fitter than ballet dancers, when they just don't know the first thing about ballet.'

'Do you do ballet?'

Millie nodded. 'I used to. Most of the girls in the team did dance at some point. It helps with the leg extensions and the grace and all that.'

'What about you?' Bailey asked Pearl. 'Did you do dance?'

Pearl felt her face redden under his gaze. He had very deep eyes, almost black. 'Um, no. No, I just swam.'

He waited, but she didn't say anything else. 'Right . . . well, tell me how you got into swimming then?'

Out of the corner of her eye, Pearl saw Evie nudge

Millie. She frowned slightly. 'Uh – well, I started swimming when I was really little.' *My dad took me every week* . . . Her throat closed up. She still couldn't say the word 'dad'. 'I went every week and I had proper lessons from when I was about three. And I just really liked going – and then when I was about seven, they started up a synchro club at my local pool, and my teacher said I should come along. And that was it, really.' She stopped again.

'What is it that you love about swimming?' Bailey asked, his voice soft and his eyes fixed on her face.

'I don't know. I just . . . I don't know.' Pearl felt helpless. How could she explain? That it was just a part of her, like an arm or a leg. That when she was in the water she felt as though she was home, as though it was where she belonged. It all sounded silly in her head, so she just shrugged. 'Sorry, I'm not very good with words.'

Bailey smiled. 'You're doing fine.'

'Well, I can tell you how it makes *me* feel,' said Millie. 'I love it because it makes me feel weightless, free, unconstrained, washed clean of all unnecessary thoughts and graceful as a dolphin.'

Pearl's jaw dropped and Evie stared at Millie. Bailey gave a short laugh, which he hastily turned into a cough. 'That's very expressive.'

Millie looked smug. 'I read a lot of books.'

Bailey coughed again, and looked down at the table. 'That's pretty much all my questions,' he said. 'Though there is one' – he hesitated – 'my editor told me to ask, but it makes me feel weird . . .'

Pearl felt intrigued. Bailey had seemed so confident up to this point – what could the strange question be?

'Go on,' said Evie. 'We can always refuse to answer.' She grinned.

'Well, it's – um . . . Oh, all right. My editor wanted to know if it was awkward for you,' he said to Pearl. 'Being a black girl on a white team. There, I've said it. I don't like asking the question.'

Pearl was surprised. 'Awkward? What do you mean?'

'Oh, something to do with synchro swimmers all being supposed to look the same. To help the synchronicity. You don't have to answer if you don't want to,' Bailey added hastily.

'I don't mind . . .' said Pearl slowly.

'It's sort of a fair question,' added Evie. 'I mean, the managers do like us all to look the same. Sometimes if one girl is darker-skinned than the others, we have to use spray tan to match.'

'You couldn't all match me, though,' said Pearl, a small smile tweaking the corner of her mouth.

Millie giggled. 'I don't think we have enough bottles of tan. I'd love to have your skin though – it's so beautiful. And it doesn't show if you blush, like mine does.'

'Yes, it does,' said Evie, watching Pearl closely. 'Look.'

Pearl, uncomfortably aware of Bailey's eyes on her yet again, shuffled in her seat. 'Anyway, it doesn't matter to me. No one's ever said anything, and I don't feel different. I mean, we're all there to do the same job. What matters is that we're *good* at it.' She suddenly realized how fierce she sounded. 'And that we work hard,' she added, hoping she hadn't come across as arrogant. Interviews were so difficult!

Bailey grinned lopsidedly. 'I get that. All that training – you could probably snap me in half with the muscles you've all got.'

Pearl saw Evie nudge Millie again, and it made her annoyed. Did they think Bailey was flirting with her or something? Feeling uncomfortable, she said sharply, 'Is that everything? Because we're on our lunch break . . .'

Instantly, Bailey looked embarrassed. He leaned forward to switch off his recorder. 'Of course, I'm really sorry. Thanks so much for coming to talk to me, I really appreciate it. Can I let you know when the article comes out?'

'If you tell Emily, she'll make sure we get a copy,' said Pearl, already out of her seat and on her way to the door.

Bailey bit his lip. Was he disappointed? Pearl felt puzzled. What was going on here? 'No problem,' he said, and cleared his throat.

'You can email me, if you like,' Evie said suddenly. 'Sometimes we don't get to hear about stuff, so let me know as well.' She reached for a pen and paper.

Pearl was astonished. What was Evie doing, giving her email address to this stranger?

'Thanks,' said Bailey. He smiled at them as they turned to go. 'And good luck!'

'Why did you give him your email?' asked Pearl as the three of them headed back down the corridor.

Evie shrugged. 'Because he wanted yours, idiot. Couldn't you tell?'

'Why would he want mine?' asked Pearl.

Evie rolled her eyes. 'He fancied you, Pearl. Don't you notice anything?'

'What?'

'He did stare at you a lot,' agreed Millie, 'and he seemed really nice.'

'But – but,' Pearl spluttered, 'what's that got to do with anything? I don't even know him!'

'Oh, live a little, Pearl,' said Evie, grinning. 'Look, I thought if he emailed me then I could give him your address. But only if you say I can.'

Pearl didn't know what to say. She looked at Millie.

'I thought he was cute,' admitted Millie. 'But don't ask me what to do. I'm useless with boys.'

'At least you've *had* a boyfriend,' said Pearl.

'Only for two weeks,' said Millie. 'And we only went out once before he dumped me. I don't think that really counts.'

Evie put up her hands. 'It's up to you,' she said to Pearl. 'But it's not like he knows where you live or anything. I mean, haven't you got Facebook friends you don't really know?'

'She's not on Facebook, remember?' said Millie.

Evie rolled her eyes again. 'I give up!'

'All right,' said Pearl suddenly. 'All right, you can give him my email address. But only if he asks. And don't tell him anything stupid, like I fancy him or stuff like that. Because I don't, OK?'

'OK,' said Evie, instantly brightening. 'I'll tell him you definitely *don't* fancy him but that you want him to have your email.'

'No!' wailed Pearl.

The other two burst out laughing. 'Your face!' giggled Millie.

'Don't worry,' said Evie. She drew a cross over her heart. 'I won't breathe a word.'

Pearl looked at her suspiciously, but Evie said nothing more about the subject. And honestly, Pearl thought to herself, her friends were making it all up. She was absolutely sure that Bailey hadn't been flirting with her. So all this about him fancying her was just nonsense.

Wasn't it?

Chapter 3

give him a chance to explain

'How was the interview?' asked Pearl's mum, Linda, as she got into the car that evening.

'Fine,' said Pearl. 'It wasn't just me, so that was good because I couldn't think of anything to say.' *Why would Bailey fancy someone who obviously can't string three words together?* She'd been trying not to think about it all afternoon.

Her mum laughed. 'Oh, bless you, darling. I'm sure it wasn't as bad as you thought.'

'It really was.'

'Never mind, you can forget about it now. Was the rest of the day all right?'

'Yeah. We did a new throw this afternoon. It's really hard, but Bonnie thinks we can do it.'

'Who's jumping this time?' asked Linda, negotiating a roundabout.

27

'Jen. She's done more than anyone; she's the most experienced.'

'I do like her,' commented Linda. 'Such a nice girl, always looking out for the rest of you.' She hesitated. 'Pearl, love, I have to tell you I heard from your dad again today.'

Pearl stiffened, feeling a coldness sweep through her. 'So?' she said sharply.

'He really wants to talk to you,' her mother went on nervously. 'He said again how much he misses you and Harrison.'

'Tough.'

Linda bit her lip. 'It's been six months, Pearl. Don't you think you could talk to him, just for a few—'

'No, I don't,' said Pearl firmly. 'After what he did to us? To you? Does he know what a state you were in? Does he know you had to get antidepressants from the doctor?'

Linda sighed. 'It's not like he's my favourite person. But he is your dad, and even if he and I – well, even if we're not together any more, he still wants to see you and be part of your life.'

'He should have thought of that before he walked out,' snapped Pearl. She couldn't explain the burning hot anger she still felt at her dad's betrayal. The one person she thought she could count on – he'd let her down, on the most brilliant day of her life. He'd let them all down, and she could never forgive him for that. No matter how much time went by, it still hurt like a stab wound.

Linda sighed again but didn't press the point, and Pearl felt mildly annoyed that her mother had even raised the subject. Had she forgotten the awful days and weeks that had followed Dad's departure? Had she forgotten the truly heartbreaking Christmas Day as a family of three instead of four? Not to mention the revelation that Dad had 'gone off with another woman' – something Pearl had hardly been able to believe. Why wouldn't he want her beautiful, kind mother any more? Why wouldn't he want to be with his own kids? They'd hoped for a while that he would change his mind, but as the weeks went by, it became obvious that he was staying away, and Pearl had hardened her heart against him. It would take more than a phone call to break through that now.

'You thought of a film for Saturday yet?' asked Linda, changing the subject. 'Harrison's going round to Tom's again. Girls' night in!'

Pearl smiled. 'I don't mind. Didn't you say there was this great eighties film you wanted to see?'

'*Mannequin!*' exclaimed her mum. 'With Andrew McCarthy! You're going to love it.'

'You're so stuck in the eighties, Mum—'

'Or *Splash*! It's about a mermaid – and it's got Tom Hanks. You like him, right?'

'Mum, he's *ancient*!'

Linda laughed ruefully. 'All right, we can watch something with Orlando Bloom in, if you insist, or Robert Pattinson. Just not *Twilight* again, please. I can't cope with any more vampires.'

'I'm completely over *Twilight*,' declared Pearl.

'Thank goodness.' Her mum looked across affectionately. 'I love our Saturday nights. You're such a good girl friend.'

Pearl smiled back. Who'd have thought that she and her mum would have grown so close? Growing up, it was always Dad who came with her to swimming competitions and asked about lessons and practices. That meant that she'd spent more time with him than with her mum. Linda had never really understood Pearl's need to be in the water for half the day. But when Dad left – Pearl's heart constricted again at the thought – she and her mum had forged a bond stronger than anything they'd had before. One good thing to come out of all the awfulness. Her mum was practically her best friend now.

'Harrison!' Linda called as they came in the front door. 'We're home!'

A thumping rhythm from upstairs indicated that Pearl's sixteen-year-old brother was already back, and 'revising' as usual.

'How can that music help him revise?' wondered Linda aloud.

'No idea,' said Pearl, but she suspected that her brother was actually practising his guitar. Harrison played in a band at school and they had a gig coming up at the end of term. He was supposed to be revising for his GCSEs but he didn't seem bothered about exams. In fact, the only things he did bother about were his music and his appearance. Pearl found him intensely irritating and sometimes wondered how they could be related. She worked so hard at her swimming and was driven to succeed, whereas Harrison only seemed driven to doss around!

'You look tired, love,' Linda commented. 'Have you eaten enough today? Let me get you a sandwich while I'm sorting out dinner.'

'Thanks, Mum. I do feel a bit tired.'

'Go and watch the television,' suggested Linda. 'I'll bring it through.'

Pearl slumped onto the sofa, exhausted. It sometimes

hit her like this, the sudden onslaught of tiredness. Training had intensified once the final team selection had been made, and although she ought to be used to it by now, the stamina required still occasionally took her by surprise. Pearl knew she was fitter than almost everyone else her age, but that didn't mean she couldn't feel utterly worn out. She switched on the TV and flicked aimlessly through the channels. *I'll just close my eyes*, she thought. *Just for a few minutes* ...

Her dreams were full of splashing sounds and a dark, friendly face, smiling at her through a watery curtain.

♥

'Five, six, seven, eight. One, TWO, three, four, FIVE, SIX, seven, eight. One, TWO, THREE ... No, no, stop! Primrose, it's *left* then *right*, OK? Do it again.'

The eight swimmers sank in unison, nose clips in place and expressions serious. Bonnie's voice carried clearly through the underwater speakers. Eight pairs of legs kicked rapidly in the air, twirling and sinking, slapping the water in a complex rhythm. Underneath the surface, the girls needed all their strength to keep themselves in the right position, and all their lung capacity to cope before taking their next breath.

There was no chatting; no banter. The girls were serious; focused; following instructions carefully. On the required count, Pearl pushed her arms down through the water hard, thrusting herself above the surface so that the whole of her upper body burst into the air. Quickly, she looked left; right; lifted her arms up sharply, then sank below the water again. The other seven girls in the line were doing exactly the same thing, she knew. She was so close to Lizzie, the girl in front, that any mistiming of the movement would result in a clashing of arms and legs.

'Good,' said Bonnie. 'Much better than yesterday. And repeat another four times. Five, six, seven, eight . . .'

Pearl's mind cleared. There was only the pool, and her body, and the other girls. Her arms sliced through the water. Her legs kicked in the air as she hung, upside-down, in the pool. She brushed water from her eyes and ears at the end of each sequence so that she could listen to Bonnie. 'No!' Bonnie cried every now and then. 'Stop, stop. Evie, you're late on that turn again. Kat, which way are you meant to be looking on count five? Then do it. Once more.'

There were no mutterings or complaints. It was over an hour before any of the girls swam to the side for a drink of water, and another hour before their feet touched solid ground. Bonnie called them out of the pool to watch the routine she'd recorded them doing. 'You need to close that gap,' she said, pointing out a pattern that wasn't quite perfect. 'Kat and Hollie-Mae, that's yours. And Pearl, your split was late there.'

Pearl nodded.

'Tomorrow,' said Bonnie, tucking her blonde hair behind her ear, 'we need to work on that moving sequence with the twists.' The girls groaned and Bonnie grinned. 'I know, I know, it's your favourite.'

'Can't we take out that look to the left that we always get wrong?' asked Kat.

Bonnie pulled a face. 'We could, but it adds to the difficulty. If we could get it right . . .'

'If we added in a second spin instead,' suggested Lizzie, 'then that would mean we could go into the jump sequence three counts later and it wouldn't matter about the look to the left.'

'Let's talk about this tomorrow,' said Bonnie. 'If you're really uncomfortable with the look to the left then we'll have to figure out a way round it.' She looked up as a woman came through the double doors onto the pool side. 'Ah, great, you're here! Girls, this is Carolina Mendoza.'

Pearl looked with interest at the newcomer. So this was the famous Spanish coach who was going to take some of their sessions for the next month! Carolina had been World Champion ten years ago and had also won an Olympic silver medal with her partner in the duet competition. The British team knew they were lucky to have engaged her. She'd coached last year's winning Spanish team to the Worlds, and she was highly respected in synchro circles, though she did have a reputation for being very strict. One of the Spanish girls had confided to Pearl at a training camp that Carolina had frightened the life out of the whole team – but she certainly got results. Gazing up at the tall, wiry, dark woman with her deep blue eyes, Pearl thought to herself that Carolina didn't look all that scary. Maybe the Spanish girls were being a bit over-dramatic.

'Pleased to meet you,' said Carolina with a smile that didn't quite reach her eyes. 'I look forward to working with you all.'

The girls murmured hellos in response.

'Right,' said Bonnie. 'I want to talk to Carolina,

so you can go and get changed. Primrose, on your way out, can you pop along to see Emily? She said something about getting your ankle signed off by the physio.'

Primrose nodded, and the girls hauled themselves out of the pool.

'What do you think?' Millie muttered to Pearl as they headed for the changing rooms. 'Of the Spanish coach, I mean?'

Pearl shrugged. 'She looks all right to me. And Emily wouldn't have asked her if she didn't think she was good.'

'I'm reserving judgement,' said Evie, joining in. 'You know what everyone says about her.'

'Not exactly everyone,' Millie pointed out. 'We know what the Spanish girls said, but maybe they were exaggerating.'

'I guess we'll find out tomorrow,' said Pearl.

They stood under the hot showers for a moment. 'Oh, have you heard from Bailey, by the way?' asked Evie suddenly.

'Who?' asked Pearl casually, pretending she didn't recognize the name.

'Oh, ha ha. The boy who interviewed us. He emailed me yesterday evening and he *did* ask for your address,' said Evie triumphantly. 'Told you he would!' She frowned. 'Didn't he email you last night?'

'Don't know,' Pearl replied, reaching for her towel. 'I didn't check my emails.'

Evie's jaw dropped. 'You didn't check . . . ? Honestly, Pearl, you're the only teenager I know who doesn't live her life online.'

'I've only got that little netbook,' said Pearl, 'and it's not like I get many emails anyway.'

'You *so* need an iPhone,' Evie told her. 'But anyway, he said he was going to email you, so you have to check them today.'

'I'll do it when I get home.' Pearl's heart gave a thump. Had Bailey really emailed her? What would he say? Was he going to ask her out? What would she say if he did?

'What's this?' asked Georgie, getting dressed nearby. Georgie was the only redhead on the team, with frizzy hair that refused to be tamed and had to be squashed into her cap by force every day. It suited Georgie, who was bouncy and chatty and loved nothing better than a good gossip. 'Who's emailing you, Pearl?'

'A boy,' Evie told her smugly. Pearl glared at her. 'You know we were interviewed yesterday? Well, it was a schoolboy and he really fancied Pearl—'

'He did not!' protested Pearl. 'You two are reading too much into it!'

'Ooh!' Georgie's eyes shone. 'A romance! Brilliant!'

'There's no romance,' insisted Pearl.

'You have to tell us *everything*,' said Georgie, grabbing Pearl's arm. She was twenty-three and her own boyfriend was away at university. 'I am completely lacking in romance of my own right now, so I have to live through others.'

Jen, overhearing, said gently, 'It's none of your business, Georgie. Pearl's still really young.'

'I had my first boyfriend at twelve, younger than Pearl,' declared Georgie.

Jen grinned. 'Yes, but Pearl's a lot more sensible than you.'

'Exactly,' agreed Hollie-Mae, nineteen and beautiful, with straight dark brown hair and velvety brown eyes. She smiled at Pearl. 'No need to rush into anything.'

Pearl felt grateful to the two of them but she wished everyone would just drop the subject! There were times when being in a group of nine girls could get claustrophobic, as everyone knew everything about everyone else. It was hard to keep a secret! *Not that Bailey's a secret*, she said to herself. *There's nothing to tell, anyway!*

But she still wondered what could be in the email.

Kat and Lizzie were the first out of the changing rooms. The twins did everything at top speed, racing each other out of the building because the first one to get to their car in the car park won the right to drive it back to their flat.

Pearl and Millie were the last to leave because they were the only ones who had to wait for their parents to pick them up. Everyone else on the team had left school, and most of them were living away from home. The twins, for example, had moved all the way down from Northumberland to live near the training centre.

Millie sat on the bench and rubbed her wispy brown hair with a towel. 'You OK today?'

'Look, I don't care if Bailey has emailed me or not,' snapped Pearl, pulling on her trainers.

'I didn't mean Bailey,' said Millie. 'I meant you. You seemed kind of worried today.'

'Oh.' Pearl glanced at her friend. 'Sorry, I thought . . . I'm all right.'

'Sure?'

Pearl sighed. 'It's nothing really. Just Dad ringing again.'

Millie instantly understood. 'I get it. He still wants to talk to you?'

'Yeah. And Mum says I should get in touch. I don't really know why – it's not like *she's* talking to him. She still can't say his name, you know – she just calls him "your father" or "your dad". But she's been going on about how he's my dad and cares about me.'

Millie raised her eyebrows. 'He didn't care about you when you got into the team.'

'Exactly!' Pearl knew her best friend would understand. 'It's like he thinks he can just come back into my life and pick up where we left off. Well, he can't.'

Millie hesitated. 'Do you think maybe you should give him a chance to explain?'

'Explain what?' asked Pearl. 'He couldn't possibly say anything that would make it all OK. I don't want to talk to him – ever. I wish he would just go away and – and die, or something.'

'Die!' Millie was shocked. 'You can't wish that, that's horrible!'

'I don't care.' Pearl looked stubborn. '*He's* horrible – what he did was horrible. He broke us all up; it's his fault. You know what it was like for my mum. She still says she could never trust another man; that he's ruined her belief in marriage and all that.'

'It hasn't been all that long though,' Millie pointed out.

'She's sworn off men for life,' Pearl went on. 'And I won't ever speak to him again. I wish he could just understand that and leave us alone.'

Millie sensibly said nothing else. The two of them gathered up their things. Pearl took a quick look around as they left the changing area. The room was empty now, the cubicles and benches quiet. Only the puddles on the floor showed that anyone had been in there. It was a strange place – a half-world between the outside and the world of water. She let the door bang behind her and followed Millie out.

As they rounded the corner to the main reception area, she nearly walked straight into her friend. 'Mills!'

'Sorry.' Millie was staring. 'I'm just surprised, that's all. After what you just said . . .'

'What are you talking about?'

'Well – that's your mum.' She pointed. 'And she doesn't look very sworn off men right now.'

Pearl's jaw dropped as she followed Millie's gaze. Sure enough, there was her mother – long black hair, pale yellow top – leaning on the reception desk and throwing her head back in a full-bellied chuckle. A white man behind the desk, tall, with greying hair at the temples, was laughing with her. As Pearl watched, he wrote something on a small card and handed it to her mum, who took it, smiling warmly at him and making a comment in a flirtatious voice.

Pearl shook her head, astonished. 'Well!' she said. 'Who's *that* then?'

Chapter 4

Bailey Ross wants to go out with me!

'Hi, darling,' said her mum as Pearl approached. She was still smiling, and Pearl saw her slip the card the man had given her into her handbag. Millie headed out of the front door, giving Pearl a wave, but Pearl was too preoccupied to wave back. She glanced suspiciously over the reception desk, but the man had gone. 'Who were you talking to?' she asked, hoping she sounded casual.

'Oh, nobody.' Linda shook her head, but her eyes still sparkled. She took Pearl's arm and said, 'Shall we go out for dinner?'

Now Pearl was really alarmed. Going out for dinner was only something that happened on special occasions. 'Why?'

'Why not?' asked her mum. 'Do I need a reason to treat my beautiful children?'

Pearl stared at her. 'Er . . .' She couldn't remember the last time she'd seen her mum so lit up from the inside. When they got to the car, she said nervously, 'Is this something to do with that man at the desk?'

Linda rifled through her handbag for the keys. 'Oh, him?' Her voice was light, but it didn't fool Pearl. 'He's one of the personal trainers in the gym. I've seen him around a couple of times, and he always smiles at me. He's got such a nice smile. He told me an awful joke – listen. There was this dog, right, and he went into a bar . . .'

'Mum . . .'

Her mother waved the keys. 'Found them!' She unlocked the car, continuing with her joke. Pearl slid into the passenger seat, only half listening. 'And then the barman said, "You can't hold your drink, can you?" Get it?'

'Um . . .'

'Dogs? Holding drinks? Oh, never mind.' Linda reversed out of the parking space, still chuckling. 'It's really bad, isn't it? I don't know why I'm laughing.' She glanced across at her daughter. 'How was training?'

'It was fine. But Mum . . .'

'What is it?' For the first time, Linda seemed to notice that Pearl wasn't laughing along. 'Are you all right, love? You look kind of down in the mouth.'

'No, no, there's nothing wrong.' Pearl gave a smile. 'Just – just curious, I suppose. I thought you said you didn't like men any more.' The words sounded childish to her own ears.

Her mum laughed. 'Oh, darling. I was only talking to him.'

'Did he – what did he give you?'

'He gave me his phone number, if you must know. What is this, the third degree?'

'Are you going to ring him?'

'I don't know!' Linda was starting to sound irritated. 'I might do. He's nice. What's wrong with that?'

Pearl said nothing. It was as though the world were turning on its head. All that stuff her mum had said about never trusting men again, about being happier without them – had she forgotten it? Those weeks she'd spent crying for Pearl's dad . . . she'd said over and over again that she'd never love anyone else, it was too painful. And here she was laughing and flirting with a strange man!

Linda obviously felt she should say something else. 'Darling, I'd never do anything to hurt you or Harrison, you know that. But maybe it's time I got myself out there again. I've been on my own for a while now.'

'You're not on your own,' said Pearl, hurt. 'You've got us.'

Linda reached out to pat her knee. 'I know, love. And you've been such a comfort to me. You've looked after me and made sure I'm all right.' She laughed. 'Almost like we've swapped places! You're my best friend, Pearl, you know that. But being with my kids isn't like being . . . with a man. Someone to go on dates with. You understand, darling?'

Pearl didn't understand. 'Yes.'

Linda smoothed her hair away from her face. 'Do you think I should have this cut? I was wondering whether I should go for a bob.'

Pearl made an effort. It was good, wasn't it, if her mum was happy? 'I think that would look nice.'

'Do you? Do you really?' Linda glanced sideways at her. 'You're not just saying that, are you? Because you've got such good judgement about these things. I won't have it cut if you don't think it would look good.'

'No, no, I do think it would look good. That's what I said.'

'Sure?'

'Yes. And if you hate it, you can always grow it out again.'

Linda reached for her hand. 'My practical daughter. What would I do without you, eh? The voice of reason, that's what you are.'

One of us needs to be, Pearl said silently in her head. *Because it sounds like you've lost it.*

♥

'Harrison!' Pearl's mum called as they let themselves into the house. 'Can you come down for a minute?'

There was no reply from Harrison's room except the usual thumping bass line.

'I don't suppose he heard me,' said Linda. 'Can you go up, love, and tell him we're all going out for dinner?'

Pearl headed up the stairs, wincing as the volume of Harrison's music increased. 'Harrison?' There was no answer, even when she knocked loudly, so she pushed the door open.

There was a scurry of books and clothes from the other side of the room. 'Don't you ever *knock?*' asked her brother furiously.

Pearl wondered what he had hidden so quickly

under the bed, but decided she didn't really want to know. 'I did knock,' she retorted. 'Loads.'

'Well, you can't come in.'

'I don't want to come in. We're going out for dinner.'

'Who is?'

'All of us – you too.'

Harrison scowled, his black brows drawing together. 'What, now?'

'Yes.' Pearl felt irritated. Why did her brother have to be so confrontational all the time?

'What for? We never go out for dinner.'

Pearl shrugged. 'Mum wants to treat us.'

Harrison still looked suspicious. 'She doesn't usually.'

This was exactly what Pearl had been thinking, but she didn't want to discuss it with him. 'Are you coming then, or what?'

'Yeah, yeah, all right. Give me a minute.'

Pearl sighed as she went downstairs. 'He's coming,' she told her mother.

Linda beamed. 'Lovely. I can't remember the last time we all went out. Shall we go to the Harvester? There's enough on the menu to suit you, isn't there?'

Pearl, like all the girls on the synchro team, had

to be careful with her diet. Carbs and protein were important, but fats and sugars could impact on her performance. 'The menu's fine there, Mum. I'll find something.'

Harrison thumped down the stairs, pulling his hood up to hide his closely cropped hair. 'Anyone would think you're embarrassed to be seen with us,' joked Linda, but Harrison merely grunted and Pearl suspected that it was very close to the truth.

The Harvester wasn't busy and they soon found a table. 'I can't remember the last time we went out for dinner,' said Linda cheerfully.

Harrison shot her an odd glance but said nothing. Pearl could tell what he was thinking. *Why is she so happy and bright this evening?* She wasn't about to tell him about the personal trainer at her gym though. Instead, she started telling her mum and brother about the new throw lift they'd added to the routine, and about the Spanish coach who had come to train them for a while. 'I've watched one of her routines on YouTube,' she added. 'Back when she was World Champion. She's brilliant – and the routines she's done for teams are amazing too.'

'You are so lucky to have such wonderful opp-ortunities,' her mum said with a sigh. 'I still can't believe my little girl is going to the Olympics. It gives me a thrill whenever I tell someone.'

Pearl smiled at her. 'Thanks, Mum. It's really weird, but in some ways I keep forgetting. I guess it's because we spend so much time training, it feels like it's going on for ever. Although every now and then we get a reminder, like an interview or a photo call or something.'

'Have you got your new costumes yet?' asked Linda. 'The ones for the free programme?'

Pearl shook her head. 'Not yet. Emily's a bit annoyed that the woman who makes them is running late. But I think she's been ill. It takes her ages to make each one specially. And they're so expensive.'

The food arrived and Harrison dug into his barbecued spare ribs without looking up. Pearl saw her mum glance at him and give a small sigh. Why couldn't Harrison join in normal conversations these days? Making an effort, Pearl asked, 'How's the rehearsals for the gig going?'

'All right,' said her brother. 'Pass the salt.'

'Are you going to be ready in time?' Pearl persisted. 'Didn't you say the other day that the singer didn't know her words?'

'Yeah. And she's a bit flaky. We're never sure if she's going to turn up. Tom knows someone else who's interested though, so we might replace her.'

'Does she know?' asked Linda. 'That you're going to kick her out, I mean.'

Harrison shrugged. 'Might do. Dunno.'

Pearl exchanged a look with her mother. It was a bit mean of the band to be talking of getting rid of their singer without letting her know, wasn't it? But she didn't want to annoy Harrison by suggesting it. An argument would spoil the meal, and she suddenly felt a rush of warmth towards her mum for suggesting it. Regardless of the real reason Linda was cheerful, it was nice to be out as a family again. A family of three, these days, but still a family . . .

'I've tried to get tickets again,' her mum broke into Pearl's thoughts. 'For the awards ceremony.'

'Any luck?'

'I shan't know for a while. It's a competition.' Linda sighed and shook her head. 'I know they had to make it fair for everyone but it seems horribly mean that I can't get a ticket to see you swim the free programme and collect a medal.'

'Mum! I won't get a medal!' Pearl laughed. 'You're crazy! We're not expecting to win anything – you know how good the other teams are!'

'Then you won't win,' said Harrison unexpectedly.

'If you keep saying you won't, then you won't.'

Pearl stared at him. 'We're not good enough.'

He rolled his eyes. 'Haven't you ever heard of thinking positive?'

Pearl was taken aback. Harrison was the last person she expected to talk about being positive! 'What do you suggest?' she asked cautiously.

'We just wrote this new song for the band,' Harrison told her, picking up fries with his fingers and dipping them in ketchup. 'It's all about expecting good stuff to happen and then it will. Like you make it happen by your mindset. And if your mindset is really pessimistic, then you'll get ill and fail your exams and stuff like that. The song's called "Mindset".'

'Wow. It sounds cool.'

Harrison's face fleetingly twitched into a smile. 'Yeah, it is.'

Pearl had forgotten just how much her brother's face changed when he smiled. It shocked her – when had she last seen him smile? Not for a long time, she realized now. Probably not since their dad had left. Harrison had wanted to go and live with Dad, but it wasn't possible: the new flat wasn't big enough, Linda had told Pearl. Besides, there was the 'other woman' to consider; from what Linda said, it didn't sound like this new woman wanted anything to do with kids.

'Can we come to your gig?' asked Linda now.

Harrison pulled a face. 'Not really, Mum. It's for the Year Elevens. It's not like a public concert. Sorry.' And he did look genuinely sorry for a moment too.

'Oh, that's a shame,' said Linda. 'I haven't heard you play for ages.'

'We might be doing a gig in the summer,' Harrison offered. 'In August.'

'August? Oh, but—' Linda stopped, then smiled. 'That would be great – just let me know when.'

Pearl knew why her mum had hesitated. August was when IT was happening – the Olympics! And that knot of excitement was back in her tummy; the one that sang quietly to itself most of the time and only occasionally burst into full-blown pride. *I'm going to be competing at the Olympics!*

♥

It wasn't until much later that evening, when Pearl had got back from the Harvester and was sitting in bed in her pyjamas, that she remembered about Bailey. Had he emailed her? She felt oddly nervous as she reached under the bed for the slim navy netbook that had been a birthday present. It was a good size to take on overseas training camps, though she usually forgot about it until she was on the plane and already on her way.

It took a moment to remember her own password. She frowned at the screen, her dark skin crinkling between her eyes. Then her expression cleared as she tapped in a sequence of numbers and letters that she'd created especially to vent her feelings about her brother after a particularly annoying encounter: Harr1s0nSt1nks!

The little netbook took only seconds to power up and Pearl opened her emails. There were two links from friends and a marketing email from the British Synchro website. There was also, right at the top, an email from an address she didn't recognize. The subject line was: *You'll probably say no*, and it was dated the day before. Was this it? Intrigued, she clicked on the message.

From: bailey007@gmail.com

Hi Pearl
We met today. I interviewed you and asked you all the questions you didn't want to answer. Sorry about that. I emailed your friend Evie earlier this evening and she gave me your email address. I hope you don't mind. She said you would be OK about it.

I've written the next bit about twenty times.
You're probably wondering why I'm writing to you
at all – or maybe strange boys write to you all the
time and you're thinking, *Oh no, not another one* – but
I just wanted to say I think you're really nice. All of
you are so amazing to be doing what you do, but I
think you're really cool and I'd sort of like to get to
know you better. I don't meet many girls who are so
dedicated to something, and it's really
interesting. I kind of feel we'd have loads to talk
about, because I'm really dedicated to writing and
we could talk about how other people don't
understand us and all that kind of thing, LOL.

If you think this doesn't sound too weird and
loopy, please do write back. I know you're on a mad
schedule and all that, but I'm sure we could find time
for a coffee or something, right?

Signing off before I write something really
thick-sounding (oops, too late).

Bailey Ross

Pearl read the email with some astonishment and
a slight flutter in her stomach. Wow! The other girls
had been right! He *did* want to go out with her! The
last line made her laugh – it was exactly how she'd
have felt if she'd sent an email like that.

Bailey Ross wants to go out with me. It was her very first, proper offer of a date. One of Harrison's friends had once made a fumbling attempt to kiss her, but she'd scared him off by lying that Harrison was very protective – as if! And of course there had been the boys she'd wanted to go out with – the ones she'd dreamed about, who always seemed to be going out with other girls or simply didn't know she existed. But this boy was real, proper – and he was nice.

Pearl leaned back and rested her head against the wall, thinking. Evie and Millie had agreed he was cute, and they obviously thought he was someone worth getting to know. She hadn't felt particularly blown away when she met him, but he'd been quite sweet in the interview. Even though she was completely tongue-tied when he asked her simple questions, he hadn't seemed to mind. And he had a friendly face, and the way he wrote made her laugh. That was a good start, wasn't it?

But how could she say yes? She had practically no spare time. She wasn't an ordinary girl, finishing school at 3.30 with only her homework to think about. She was an Olympic swimmer, and that brought so many other things to her life – the hours of training, the overseas camps, the extra events. Bailey might think it was easy to find time for coffee, but was it? Some

56

of the other girls on the team had boyfriends and they were always complaining about how difficult it was to see them. Bailey was at school during the day, so that would mean trying to meet in the evenings, and Pearl had to make sure she got the right amount of sleep and ate at the right times and things like that. Wouldn't dating just make her life even more complicated?

Plus, what about her mum? Pearl knew Linda loved spending time with her. They both looked forward to their weekends, watching girlie films or sometimes going shopping together. How would her mum feel if Pearl started going on dates and she was left home alone?

Pearl couldn't deny that the idea of meeting up with Bailey had some appeal, but she wasn't sure she actually fancied him. She hadn't looked at him and gone 'Wow!', had she? Weren't you supposed to feel like that about people you dated?

It was all so difficult! She wondered if she should ask Millie and Evie for their advice, but instinctively she knew what they would say: 'Go for it!' and 'What have you got to lose?' and other such phrases. They would be really excited for her, and she'd have to tell them all about it afterwards . . .

Pearl suddenly felt very nervous. She didn't feel old

enough to have a boyfriend! She only knew about swimming, nothing about boys! Before she could change her mind, she typed:

Hi Bailey
Thanks for your email. Sorry, I don't really have time for dates at the moment, but thanks for asking. No one has ever asked me before!

She hesitated and then deleted the last sentence. Should she put something about not wanting to hurt his feelings? 'I hope you don't mind'? No, that sounded stupid – of course he would mind, wouldn't he? Or maybe he was just asking her on the off-chance that she'd say yes. Maybe – a horrible thought struck her – maybe he was just asking her out because she was in the Olympics and sort of famous.

No, surely Bailey wasn't like that? She looked down at the netbook again and added a bit more.

Hi Bailey
Thanks for your email. Sorry, I don't really have time for dates at the moment, but thanks for asking. It was really sweet of you.
Best wishes,
Pearl

She clicked 'send' and immediately wished she could take it back. Had she been tactful enough? Maybe she should have explained a bit more why she was turning him down? Had she even done the right thing?

For some light relief, she clicked on one of the YouTube links a friend had sent and laughed at a cat having a fight with a computer printer. Someone had done a voiceover for the cat. Pearl marvelled at the time it must have taken. Some people must have hours and hours to fill with making videos like this! For a tiny moment she wished she had more spare time, but that would mean giving up the team, and that was unthinkable. Synchro was her life; her passion. Nothing was more important than that.

Chapter 5

she's not tough, she's horrible

Pearl had been looking forward to the team's first session with Carolina. It was always exciting to be coached by someone unfamiliar – you never knew what they might ask of you and it was good for the team to be challenged. But she felt a little nervous as they arrived on the poolside. Carolina didn't smile and say 'Good morning' like Bonnie always did. Instead, she nodded curtly at them and gestured towards the pool. 'Get in and warm up,' she said. 'Then we'll get started.'

The girls obediently dived into the pool and began their lengths. Pearl found herself thinking of Bailey and the email she'd sent the night before. How would he react when he received it? Would he be gutted or would he simply shrug and forget her? Powerfully, her arms sliced through the water, her regular breaths coming automatically. Her mind churned at its own pace, little voices niggling at her. She wished she could be better with words. The message she'd sent seemed rude and ungrateful now.

When the girls had completed their warm-up lengths, they swam to the side of the pool to listen to Carolina. 'I have watched your recorded practices,' she told them, her eyes quickly switching from one girl to the next. 'We have much work to do. You are very sloppy.'

The girls exchanged glances. Pearl felt hurt. They knew they weren't the best in the world, but they'd made enormous progress over the past two years, and calling them all 'very sloppy' wasn't a good way to get the team on side.

'You,' said Carolina suddenly, pointing a manicured talon at Pearl. 'Your mistakes stand out more because of your skin. You have to work twice as hard to be perfect.'

Pearl's jaw dropped, and she heard a gasp to her left.

Carolina noticed the reaction. 'It is true,' she said, shrugging. 'I do not say it is right, but it is what people can see.'

Pearl felt as though she wanted to say something, to retort, but her mind was churning with outrage and she couldn't think properly. For the second time in twenty-four hours she wished she were good with words.

'So,' said Carolina, 'we begin. A straight line please.'

For the next two hours, she grilled them on basic manoeuvres, making them perform over and over again, in different patterns and sequences. She allowed no discussion; no comments. She was ruthless and cruel in her feedback, picking on Evie for being behind so many times that Evie's eyes filled with tears. 'There is no room for mistake,' she kept saying. 'You make mistake, you lose. It is simple.'

Pearl worked hard, her mind entirely focused on the task. The exercises set were good, but the way the coach treated them was humiliating. One by one, they were picked apart until every single girl was fuming. Pearl's gaze flicked more than once towards Bonnie, who sat watching with an unreadable expression. *Why isn't she stepping in to back us up?* Pearl thought furiously as she trod water, a fixed smile on her face. *She must be able to tell we all hate this Spanish woman, so why isn't she telling her to be nicer to us?*

Only when the clock showed ten minutes past twelve did Bonnie rise to her feet and mutter to Carolina. Carolina looked surprised. 'Already? But we are in the middle of something. Cannot we just move lunch?'

'No,' said Bonnie firmly. 'They must have their two hours.'

Carolina raised her eyes to the distant ceiling. 'Whatever you say. Girls, lunch time.' She put down the microphone and turned to Bonnie. 'Where is there a place I can find lunch?'

Bonnie explained about the local facilities as the nine girls hauled themselves out of the pool. She ignored their dark looks as they headed to the change area.

'Not even a "well done"!' said Millie in a vehement whisper as they walked along the pool.

The other girls waited until they were in the changing room before bursting into aggrieved complaints. 'Good grief, what a poisonous woman!' cried Georgie. 'She's like Hitler in a swimming costume!'

'Did you hear what she said to Pearl?' asked Hollie-Mae, her beautiful dark eyes narrowing indignantly. 'It was practically racist!'

Pearl felt grateful to Hollie-Mae for saying something she wasn't sure she could say herself. But Pearl knew she was by no means the only one to have been singled out during the practice.

'Did you hear what she said about *me*?' fumed Kat.

'That she thought my legs weren't actually the same length because I couldn't kick in time on the left side!' Lizzie giggled but turned it into a hasty cough when Kat glared at her.

'She's the worst coach we've ever had,' said Evie vehemently. Several of the others nodded and agreed.

'She's not the *worst* coach,' said Jen reasonably, trying to calm the situation. 'She's just the rudest. The stuff she made us do was actually kind of good.'

'Except she was ridiculously precise!' objected Lizzie. 'I mean, we all know we have to be synchronized, but she was even comparing our *toes*! And I did *not* have my little finger sticking out during that arm movement.'

Pearl looked round at her friends, their faces flushed and furious. The changing room buzzed with anger and hardly anyone had bothered to get their towels out yet. She caught Millie's eye, and her best friend pulled a face. Millie was keeping quiet, though she had also come in for her fair share of criticism – not to mention the scathing comments Carolina had made about being a team reserve.

'I guess this is why Spain wins all the medals,' said Jen with a resigned shrug. 'We'll just have to shut up and get on with it.'

'You can't mean that,' said Primrose, her pale face

64

flushed. Primrose seldom offered an opinion unless she felt very strongly. 'She's meant to be with us for ages. She'll drive us all mad.'

'But she'll make us a better team,' argued Jen.

'No, she won't,' said Georgie, her red hair springing out from her head as she took off her cap. 'She'll make us all hate swimming so much we won't want to get it right for her. Coaching isn't just about criticizing. Did she once, just *once*, say "good" to anything we did?'

There was a slight pause as everyone tried to remember. Pearl rubbed her legs with a towel and looked at the floor. Seeing everyone so upset made her miserable.

'No,' said Jen at last. 'I know, she's tough.'

'She's not tough, she's horrible,' said Hollie-Mae with a shudder. 'I can't do a month with her. I'll be ill.'

Jen looked at her sternly. 'You can't just pull a sickie if you have to work with someone you don't like.'

'I wouldn't pull a sickie,' said Hollie-Mae defiantly. 'I'd actually be ill. She's given me a headache already.'

'That's because you're hungry,' said Georgie.

'No it isn't, it's because I've been shouted at all morning.' Hollie-Mae's eyes filled with tears.

'You're not the only one,' pointed out Evie. 'How d'you think I feel, being told I'm completely unmusical and have no sense of rhythm?'

'That's enough,' said Jen. 'I'll talk to Emily, OK? Maybe she can say something to Carolina.'

'She'd better,' grumbled Kat, 'or she'll have a mutiny on her hands.'

Pearl kept silent, but privately she agreed with Kat. It was horrible to be told you were useless and no good at the thing you loved doing. No wonder the Spanish girls had all been frightened of Carolina. How could they work like this?

♥

The rest of the day did nothing to improve the girls' mood, and by home-time they were all snapping at each other. Bonnie was in despair in the afternoon practice session. 'It's like you're all thunderclouds waiting to burst,' she said, but she waved away any criticism of the Spanish coach. 'It's Emily's call,' she said, 'not mine. And Carolina was world number one, so she knows what she's doing.'

Pearl had accidentally knocked Millie's clothes onto the floor in the changing room, which made them wet and Millie cross. 'I'm sorry,' Pearl said, but they were all too tired and fed up, and Millie snapped, 'You're so clumsy, Pearl,' which made everything worse.

It wasn't often that Pearl hated training, but she was very glad when it was time to go home, and she headed out into the reception area. She was brought up short by the sight of her mum sitting on one of the squashy sofas with the same man she'd seen yesterday. Linda's eyes were bright, and she was laughing again. He was smiling too – a charming smile, with a small dimple in one cheek. He added something that Pearl couldn't hear, and Linda leaned forward and touched his knee briefly, saying, 'You can't say things like that!' in a mock-serious tone.

Pearl felt her throat close with nerves. That man again! She stomped over to the sofa and said pointedly, 'Hello, Mum.'

Linda looked up. 'Pearl, darling! I didn't see you come out.'

'Oh, really?' Pearl didn't mean to sound sharp, but she was so wound up from the day that she just wanted to get home.

Her mother was flustered. 'Pearl, this is Edward. You remember I told you he's a personal trainer.' She said it in an awed voice that annoyed Pearl further. What was so great about being a personal trainer?

Edward got to his feet in one fluid motion. Up

close, he was taller than Pearl remembered. His hair was greying slightly but he was in good shape and he couldn't have been that much older than her mother.

'Hi, Pearl.' He put out his hand. 'It's great to meet you.'

Pearl had no option but to shake his hand, but she could think of nothing polite to say. She wanted to be nice, but the smile wouldn't come. Edward's hand was strong and powerful and she felt a quiver of fear in her stomach. *I've just got used to Dad not being around*, she thought to herself. *I'm not ready for Mum to find another man – and surely she isn't either?*

Her mother stood up, reaching for her bag and overbalancing slightly. 'Whoops!'

Edward reached out a hand to steady her. 'Whoa, watch it there.'

'I promise I haven't been drinking,' Linda said, with a laugh.

'Oh, really?' He smiled.

'Well, maybe just one or two in the afternoon . . .'

Pearl, who knew perfectly well her mother never touched alcohol, listened in disbelief. She was making a complete idiot of herself! 'We should go, Mum,' she said.

Linda's face fell slightly. 'Yes, of course. You look tired, darling.'

'I am.'

'Right, then. Er . . .' She seemed at a loss to know how to say goodbye, but Edward stepped in smoothly.

'I enjoyed our chat,' he said, smiling.

Linda beamed back. 'Me too.'

'Talk to you soon. Bye, Pearl.'

'Bye.' Pearl had already turned away.

As they headed to the car, Linda had to hurry to keep up with her daughter. 'What's the matter? Is everything all right?'

'Fine,' snapped Pearl. 'Just fine.'

Her mother asked, 'Did you have a bad session today? You seem all out of sorts.'

'Yes,' said Pearl. 'The Spanish coach is horrible.'

'Oh, darling, what a shame. And you were so looking forward to it. I can't have lost my keys again – hang on . . .' Linda reached deeper into her bag. 'Ah – here they are!'

The central locking clicked, and Pearl wrenched open the door, flinging her bag into the footwell.

'Maybe you just got off on the wrong foot today,' suggested her mother, sliding into the driver's seat. 'Maybe tomorrow will be better.'

'No,' said Pearl bluntly. 'It won't. Mum, tell me, do you – do you fancy that man?'

Linda glanced at her, open-mouthed. 'That man? You mean Edward?'

'Yes, him. Edward.' Pearl clasped her hands in her lap. She knew she was being irrational, but having listened to her mum ranting about men for the past six months, she found this sudden turnaround overwhelming.

Linda made a sort of mumbling noise and then said, 'Well, a bit. He is gorgeous, don't you think?'

'*Mum*.'

'What's the matter?' Her mother frowned. 'What's all this about?'

Pearl took a deep breath. 'You said you didn't want another man. You said you couldn't believe you'd wasted so many years on Dad; that it wasn't worth it.'

'Not all men are like your dad,' said Linda quietly. 'And as I said to you before, maybe it's time I gave someone else a chance.' She shot a glance at Pearl and frowned. 'Is there something about Edward that you don't like? Is that it?'

'The way he smiles. He was kind of over-friendly.'

'Over-friendly?' Linda raised her eyebrows. 'Don't you think you're being a bit sensitive?'

'No.'

Linda was silent for a moment. 'Pearl, darling,

I wouldn't upset you for the world. But he's the first man I've even looked at since your dad left.'

'That doesn't mean you have to go out with him!'

'No . . .'

'Mum – I just have a really bad feeling about this.' Pearl gazed her mother beseechingly. 'Please.'

Linda patted her arm. 'All right, darling. I can see this means a lot to you.'

Pearl smiled in relief. 'Thanks, Mum.'

Linda put the car in gear. 'You're the most important person in my life, sweetheart. You and Harrison. I promise I won't rush into anything.' She nodded. 'I'll take things slowly.'

Pearl's heart sank. She gazed out of the window and bit her lip. There was nothing she could say.

♥

Pearl felt so tired out, she took herself off to bed early. To her surprise, there was an email waiting for her from Bailey.

Hi Pearl
Thanks for your reply. It was worth asking! ;-) Don't ask, don't get, my dad's always said, and you are pretty fit ;-) Guess you're out of my league!!

Pearl gave a snort of laughter. At least she needn't have worried about Bailey being hurt by her rejection!

On a completely unrelated thing, a mate is having a party on Saturday and I wondered if you'd like to come. Not with me – well yes, with *me*, but not *with me* with me . . . Oh blast, I'm supposed to be good with words!!

Anyway, it should be a really good night and obviously it would ~~up my cred a million points if I showed up with you~~ be completely no-strings-attached, just going as friends.

I know you've got loads of training and that, but surely they let you have an evening off every now and then?! (Besides, I know you don't train Saturday evenings.)

Have I convinced you yet?

Bailey

Pearl was smiling by the time she finished reading. Bailey could be very funny! She liked the way he wrote, as though he was actually in the room, talking to her. For a moment she was tempted. But Saturday night . . . She and Mum usually had a girlie night in. They made popcorn and watched a chick flick. Mum would be disappointed if she said she was going out. And what if it was a really late one? She couldn't afford to waste time and energy on things that weren't swimming.

Besides, going to a party with Bailey . . . she shook her head. It was obvious he still wanted to go out with her. People would assume they were together. She didn't want anyone to get the wrong impression. He was nice, yes, but she didn't fancy him. Wouldn't it be mean to make him think she did?

No. A party of people she didn't know, escorted by a boy who fancied her when she didn't fancy him? It would be a really bad idea. But she couldn't exactly say that, of course. Pearl frowned for a moment and thought hard. Then she wrote:

Hi Bailey
Really sorry. Saturday night is girls' night here. My brother goes out and mum and me always do pizza and popcorn and watch a film. She looks forward to it! And we've got this Saturday's film all sorted.
    Thanks for asking though. Hope you have a good time.
    Pearl

This time, her finger hovered over 'send' for more

than a minute. A small voice inside her head was saying, *Why don't you get out more? Swimming is important but don't you feel you're missing out on other stuff? Girls your age go to parties; they have dates; they do ordinary things. Just because you're an Olympic athlete doesn't mean you shouldn't do those things too.*

But the louder voice was saying, *Why would you want to go to a party where you don't know anyone? You go out with the girls from the team sometimes. You have fun, don't you? And who says everyone has to do the same things?*

'Not just that,' Pearl said out loud, 'but Mum *does* look forward to our girlie Saturday nights, and she'd be gutted if I went out instead.'

She clicked 'send'.

Chapter 6

will we all be thrown out?

'I'm going out with Edward on Saturday night,' Linda said in a casual voice at breakfast the next day, though her face flushed as she spoke.

Pearl was astonished. 'You're what?'

'Going out with Edward.' Her mother avoided her gaze.

'Who's Edward?' asked Harrison, still in his boxers and spooning Weetabix into his mouth as though a world shortage had been announced.

Pearl hesitated, glancing at her mum. So she hadn't said anything to Harrison yet?

'He's – he's someone I met at the centre where Pearl swims,' Linda said, rearranging the place mats on the table and not looking at anyone. 'He's a personal trainer. He's nice.'

Harrison's jaw dropped. 'You're going on a *date*?'

Linda shrugged. 'Yes. Why not?'

Harrison was speechless. After a moment he turned back to his cereal.

Pearl felt hurt. 'But Saturday night is our girlie night. You always say how much you look forward to it.' *And I turned down a party because of it!*

'And I do,' Linda replied. 'But Edward asked me out . . .'

There was a moment's silence. 'Oh,' said Pearl. There was a terrible gnawing feeling in her stomach, a knot of anxiety. They didn't even know Edward – what was he like? They'd just got used to being a family of three! Why did Mum want to mess it all up by bringing a new man into things?

Harrison finished his breakfast, dumped his bowl in the sink and went upstairs without another word. For a second Pearl envied his ability to just stomp around in a mood, not caring what others thought.

'Do you think he's mad at me?' Linda asked, her eyes creased with worry. 'I only want the best for you two, you know that, don't you?'

'Yes, Mum.'

Linda pushed her hands through her hair and sighed. 'It's so hard being a mother. I get it wrong all the time.'

'No, you don't.'

'And Harrison hardly talks to me any more.'

'He hardly talks to anyone,' Pearl pointed out. 'It's not just you.'

'You know his science teacher said his grades have gone right down this year,' her mother went on. 'He used to be top of the class – you know how bright he is. But lately it's like he just doesn't care. His teachers are all worried he's not doing enough revision.'

Pearl bit her lip. It was almost as though she and her brother were opposites. Dad leaving had made Pearl throw herself into her swimming, desperate to be even better; to work even harder – like she had to prove she didn't need his praise any more. Whereas Harrison had sort of given up; had decided nothing mattered any more.

'He needs a man about the house,' said Linda with a sigh. 'A bit of male guidance.'

Pearl was alarmed. 'You don't mean Edward?'

'No, of course not. It's far too early to think about things like that. But I can't stand up to Harrison like your dad did.' Linda made a frustrated noise. 'Look what he's done to us all! I keep telling him, but he still doesn't get it!'

'You've spoken to him again, then,' said Pearl.

'Yes – because he hasn't signed the papers my solicitor sent him. I don't understand him any more. It feels like he's doing his best to make this as hard as possible for us.' Linda reached out to stroke her daughter's hair. 'I do understand why you don't want to talk to him, darling. He's so aggravating!'

Pearl gave a half-smile. It wasn't because her dad was aggravating that she didn't want to see him. It was because she was horribly afraid she might break down and cry and tell him how much she'd missed him and beg him to come back. Or the opposite might happen – she would just yell and yell at him until he went away again. She felt her jaw tighten. It would serve her dad right if her lovely mum went out with a new man! 'I think you *should* go on a date with Edward,' she said suddenly.

Her mum looked at her hopefully. 'You do? You'd be all right about it?'

'Yes.' *Especially if it means Dad feels bad*. Pearl knew this wasn't a good reason for her mum to go out with Edward, but she didn't care. 'I mean, it's just one date, isn't it?'

'Exactly.' Linda brightened. 'We're just going out for dinner; have a chat and all that.'

'Well, that's OK then. You need a bit of a treat,' Pearl said, feeling like their roles were weirdly reversed. 'You could have your hair cut too.'

Linda beamed. 'What a brilliant idea. Thanks, girl friend.' She gave Pearl a hug.

Pearl hugged her back, trying to ignore the tiny voice that said this wasn't a good idea.

♥

By Friday, the irritation with the Spanish coach was growing. The girls grumbled as they changed into their swimming costumes. 'We've got *her* again this morning,' said Kat, pulling a face. Pearl knew just how she felt. Normally she looked forward to that first plunge into the pool, the satisfying breaking of the surface. But today she just felt nervous and tense. What would Carolina find to complain about today? And who would be first in the firing line?

'Spanish Hitler,' replied Georgie.

'Don't say that,' Jen told her sharply. 'It's really offensive.'

'Well, *she's* really offensive,' retorted Georgie. 'We shouldn't have to work with her.'

'Can't you talk to Emily again?' asked Lizzie.

Jen pulled a face. 'You know what she'll say. Carolina was a top-ranking swimmer, we're lucky to have her; we don't have to like her, we just have to do what she says, blah blah.'

A gloomy silence followed this. 'Well, I think it stinks,' declared Georgie, jamming her hat onto her head.

Pearl was inclined to agree. And to think they'd all assumed the Spanish team was exaggerating about Carolina's strict regime! Guest coaches were usually such fun, giving the girls a new perspective on things and coming up with new ideas. Carolina just made them all depressed and fed up!

'Late again, Evie!' commented Carolina in a tart voice an hour later, as the girls performed a kick sequence. 'I'm tired of saying it!'

'Then don't,' muttered Evie under her breath so that only Pearl heard her.

She glanced at her friend in concern. *Keep it together, Evie, keep it together*.

The morning went from bad to worse. Even Jen, who was the most technically proficient, came in for her fair share of criticism. 'Your elbow is not the same height as everyone else,' Carolina told her. 'You do not concentrate.'

Jen, who never let her focus drop, bit her lip and lowered her eyes.

The team's anger grew, and it began to show in

their swimming. Movements became sharper, and more than once Pearl narrowly missed being kicked underwater. Then she herself, swinging her arm backwards, caught Hollie-Mae on the side of her head and the girl let out a high yelp.

'Pearl!' snapped Carolina. 'You are not careful!'

'I'm so sorry.' Pearl turned to Hollie-Mae. 'Are you OK?'

A hand clamped to her left ear, Hollie-Mae grimaced. 'Give us a sec.'

'Do it again,' instructed the Spanish coach.

'Hang on a minute,' called Pearl. 'We're not ready.'

'*Now*, come on,' said Carolina, clicking her fingers irritably. 'And five, six, seven, eight—'

'I said we're not ready,' repeated Pearl crossly. 'Hollie-Mae's hurt.'

'It's OK, it's wearing off.' Hollie-Mae rubbed her head.

'If you get hit in a routine,' Carolina told them, 'you cannot stop to feel sorry for yourself. You must continue.'

'We do actually *know* that,' said Kat. 'But we're not doing a performance.'

'Every practice is a performance,' said Carolina, thumping the bench for emphasis.

'That's just stupid,' said Evie. Pearl caught her breath. Surely Evie knew better than to be rude to Carolina!

The coach's eyes narrowed. 'Don't talk back to me.'

'We do know what we're doing, you know.' Now that she'd started, Evie didn't seem to be able to stop. 'We *are* trying our hardest.'

'Evie . . .' muttered Pearl, trying to reach for her friend's arm. 'Evie, leave it . . .'

'Not hard enough,' snapped Carolina. 'And you do *not* know what you are doing. That's why I am here; to push you to be better.'

'You can push someone *too* far, you know,' said Evie angrily, ignoring Pearl's hand.

Carolina stood up. 'You are right. Get out.'

The girls gasped. 'What?' asked Evie, her face paling under her swim cap.

'Get out of the water. I do not want you in the team this morning if you speak to me that way.'

Evie's lips tightened. Without another word, she swam to the side and pulled herself out in one easy movement.

'Don't get changed,' Carolina told her. 'You sit on the side and watch. And keep silent.'

Evie sat there, staring at the water. Pearl didn't

know where to look. She felt an intense anger against the coach, but she wasn't brave enough to stand up to her like Evie. She gazed at her friend, willing her to look up so that she could signal sympathy, but Evie's eyes were fixed on the surface of the pool, and her face was red.

'Back into formation,' Carolina ordered, turning her back on Evie. The girls obeyed, Millie slipping in to take Evie's place in the line.

For the rest of the session, the girls worked entirely in silence. As though in unspoken support of Evie, not one of them said a word to Carolina, although they performed all her tasks as best they could. The Spanish coach seemed to like it this way and her voice became even more authoritative. *She thinks she's won*, thought Pearl to herself as she hung upside-down in the water, waiting for the count. *She thinks she's beaten us into submission.* From a sneaked glance at Evie every now and then, Pearl could see tears running down her face, and she felt awful. No one should be treated like that. She wanted nothing more than to get out of the pool so that she could comfort her friend, but she didn't dare. Pearl knew there was likely to be an explosion when the girls returned to the changing rooms.

Sure enough, when the time came to get out, they all filed silently into the changing area before turning as a group to face Jen.

Jen held up her hands. 'I know, I know. It can't go on.'

Evie burst into sobs, her whole body shaking. Pearl put her arms around her friend and looked fiercely at Jen. 'We have to say something.' She minded more about the hurt Evie was feeling than the remarks she herself had received. It made her feel so angry.

'We all have to go and see Emily,' said Kat, her face stony. 'It's completely unacceptable.'

'It's bullying, that's what it is,' added Lizzie. 'Picking on us and making us feel worthless.'

'I was doing my best,' hiccupped Evie.

'We know – it's not your fault.' Lizzie patted her on the arm. 'If it hadn't been you, it would have been someone else.'

Pearl offered Evie her towel and Evie wiped her eyes on it. 'Carolina was out of order,' Pearl told her. 'She can't do things like that; it's not fair.'

'Right,' said Jen, coming to a decision. 'Get changed, everyone, and when we're all ready, we'll go find Emily and tell her we refuse to work with Carolina any more.'

The girls nodded, but Primrose, paler than usual against her ash-blonde hair, looked worried. 'Can we do that? I mean, they've paid her a lot of money to come . . .'

'I'm not working with her again,' said Kat firmly, and there was a chorus of agreement. 'They can chuck me out of the team but I won't be bullied like that.'

Pearl gasped. 'Chuck you out of the team! They wouldn't do that, would they?' She looked around. 'If we complain – will we all be thrown out?'

'Of course not,' Jen replied. 'They can't throw out a whole team. There isn't time to train up a new one, and besides, for the first time ever, we actually stand a chance of winning a medal.'

She sounded so confident that Pearl was reassured. 'Are you sure?'

Jen nodded. 'If we all stand together, we're much stronger. Emily will have to listen to us.'

♥

Emily didn't look surprised to see the nine girls lining up in front of her. 'We need to talk to you,' said Jen, as the automatic spokesperson. 'It's about Carolina.'

Emily's gaze ranged over the girls, and she sighed. 'I thought it might be. I'm so sorry this isn't working out. I had hoped things would settle down.'

'She's bullying us,' put in Kat.

Emily looked uncomfortable. 'That's a very strong accusation, Kat. I don't think it's as bad as that.'

There was an immediate outcry. 'She made Evie get out of the pool and watch the session because she answered back,' Jen told her once she could get a word in edgeways.

Emily frowned. 'That doesn't sound . . .' She sighed again. 'All right. I'll talk to Bonnie and see what I can do.'

'We won't work with her again,' said Kat, her voice tight. 'Just so you know. We're all agreed. If she takes the practice, we won't do it.'

Emily paused for a moment. 'Thank you for your feedback,' she said politely. 'It's Friday, so I shall get back to you on Monday.'

'But—'

'That's the end of the discussion,' said Emily firmly.

Pearl followed the others out, feeling somewhat disappointed. She wasn't sure what she'd expected – a yelling match or for Emily to simply say they were quite right and Carolina would be fired then and there.

The others seemed to feel the same way. 'She could at least have said she was on our side,' grumbled Georgie.

'But she can't,' pointed out Hollie-Mae. 'She has to do what's best for the team as a whole.'

'What's best for the team is for that woman to be sent packing,' said Kat vehemently, and they all agreed.

'Well, we've done what we can,' said Jen, 'so there's no point going on about it. We've got Bonnie this afternoon for the routine work, and I'm late for a physio appointment. And tomorrow's Saturday so we're in the gym anyway. We have to let it go. You know what it's like trying to swim when you're all het up.'

'You know what we should do?' said Millie as she, Pearl and Evie headed off to the cafeteria. 'We should go out on Sunday – shopping or something. Take our minds off it. What do you think?'

Evie looked grumpy. 'I don't feel like it.'

'I think it's a really good idea,' said Pearl. Her spirits automatically lifted at the thought of a day out with her friends. 'We haven't been out for ages.'

'We could go and see a film,' said Millie.

'We could go to Starbucks,' added Evie, her expression suddenly more cheerful. 'And have an enormous, completely-not-allowed caramel latte with hazelnut syrup and whipped cream.'

The other two laughed. 'That sounds disgusting,' said Pearl. Then she remembered how upset her friend had been. She linked arms with Evie. 'But if that's what you want, that's what you should have!'

♥

Pearl had a text from her mum in the afternoon.

Can you get lift with Millie today? Am a bit tied up. X

Millie nodded. 'That's fine.' It wasn't that unusual for the girls to share lifts sometimes, since they both lived in the same direction from the fitness centre. Pearl thought nothing of it until she got home.

There was a man's jacket hanging on the coat peg by the door. Pearl wouldn't have noticed it if it hadn't been sticking out a bit. She felt suddenly sick before she realized it wasn't Dad's. But who . . . ?

She had been quiet coming in, and so when she walked into the sitting room, the two people were still kissing on the sofa. Pearl froze to the spot, her hands icy and her stomach churning. 'Mum!'

Her mother's head jerked up, and she pulled away from Edward as though she'd suddenly been electrocuted. 'Pearl! Oh God! I – er – I didn't hear you come in!'

Pearl wanted to make a cutting remark, but her throat had closed up and she was unable to speak.

Edward looked momentarily confused, his greying hair ruffled and his eyes unfocused. Then he smiled. 'Hi again, Pearl. Sorry if we startled you.'

Startled me? How about giving me a heart attack? Pearl simply stared at him.

Linda, flushed and trying to avoid an awkward silence, began babbling. 'Did you have a good day, love? Shall I make you a cup of tea? Dinner's in the oven; I made a lasagne and there's some salad in the fridge. Er – Edward's not staying for dinner . . . he – uh – he just came over this afternoon to spend some time . . .'

'I thought you were going out tomorrow evening,' said Pearl icily.

'Oh, we are, we are.' Linda glanced desperately at

Edward. 'This afternoon was a – er – a bit of a last-minute thing.'

'I rang your mum at lunch time and said I had the afternoon off,' Edward said smoothly. 'And she was free too, so I came over.'

Here. You came over here. And snogged my mum on our sofa in our sitting room, right where Dad used to do the same thing. Before he walked out on her and left her a miserable wreck. Pearl glared. 'Oh.' Her previous idea that Dad might be hurt by Mum going out with someone new now seemed incredibly pointless. *I should never have encouraged her.*

'But I should probably be going now,' added Edward, getting to his feet. 'I can imagine it's a bit awkward for you.'

A bit awkward?

Edward leaned over to kiss Linda goodbye. She offered her cheek nervously, watching Pearl. 'Thanks for this afternoon.'

He smiled at her. 'I had a great time.'

I bet you did. Suddenly Pearl wanted to be alone; to get away from this situation, which was making her feel as though she wanted to throw up. She opened her mouth to say something, but couldn't think of the words, so simply turned and went upstairs, noting automatically that Harrison's room was silent – meaning he was out of the house and probably round at a mate's. *The perfect opportunity for Mum to bring round her boyfriend ... eurgh.* She closed the door firmly behind her and stared glumly at the carpet.

What a truly revolting day.

Chapter 7

chat to Bailey?

There was a quiet tap.

'Come in,' said Pearl reluctantly.

Her mum stuck her head round the door. 'Hi, darling. Is it – can we talk?'

Pearl looked away. 'I guess.'

Linda came into the room, hesitant. She perched on the edge of Pearl's desk and looked at her daughter, sitting on her bed with her back to the wall. 'I'm very sorry about earlier,' she said, her gaze flicking to Pearl's face and away again. 'I didn't mean for you to – see us.'

Pearl shrugged, trying to pretend it didn't matter. 'It's none of my business.'

'No, it *is* your business,' said Linda. 'I don't want to upset you. I know it was a bit of a shock.' Her expression became dreamy. 'He's just so lovely.'

Pearl didn't know what to say, so she kept quiet.

'He really is,' insisted Linda. 'He kept saying he would only come to the house if I was completely certain about it. He wanted to meet in town – he said he didn't want to make me uncomfortable.'

'Good for him,' said Pearl in an I-couldn't-care-less voice.

'And then . . . well, one thing just led to another . . .' Linda giggled suddenly in a girlish way. 'You know what it's like.'

No, Mum, actually I don't, Pearl wanted to say. *And I wouldn't snog some boy I hardly knew and bring him back to the house. It's just wrong!*

'Anyway' – her mum stood up – 'he's invited us all to go on a picnic on Sunday.'

'Sunday?' Pearl stared. 'I can't. I'm going out with Millie and Evie.'

Linda's face fell. 'You didn't say.'

'We only decided today. We had such a bad morning with Carolina, and Evie was really upset.'

Linda sat down again. 'What happened?'

Pearl told her about the training session and how they'd all marched into Emily's office to tell her they wouldn't work with Carolina any more.

'Pearl!' Linda was alarmed. 'Can you do that? I mean, Emily is the team manager. She should know what's best for the team.'

'Well, she doesn't,' Pearl said. 'Not this time. And everyone's really angry about it. And so you see, Millie and I have to take Evie out for a bit, because she was so upset.'

Her mum nodded. 'I do understand, darling.' She paused for a moment. 'Could we do both? I – I don't want to push you into things, but I would like you to get to know Edward a bit.' She bit her lip. 'I really like him, Pearl. He makes me laugh, and he's so kind and thoughtful. Not a bit like – like your dad.'

Pearl looked at her, torn. She really wanted to go out with her friends, but it wasn't often that Mum asked her to do something these days. 'I don't know . . .'

'How about this,' said Linda, sitting forward. 'You go out with your friends in the morning and have lunch out. Harrison and I could go to the supermarket and pick up some things for the picnic, then come by the shopping centre and meet you later. Then we could all go on to the park for tea. We'll just make it tea instead of lunch; I'm sure Edward won't mind.'

Pearl hesitated. 'I suppose so. I'll have to let the others know.'

'Of course. See what they say. But I'd really love us

to have a proper meet-up. Us three, and Edward and his son.'

'His son?' Pearl sat bolt upright. 'He has a *son* too?'

Her mother looked embarrassed. 'Oh, didn't I tell you? Edward's divorced – he's got a son about your age from his first marriage.'

Pearl's jaw dropped. This was getting way too complicated! Now Edward had a *son* to bring into the mix? How was that going to work? 'Mum . . .'

'Darling, anyone my age is going to come with baggage,' said Linda hastily, as though hoping to forestall any argument Pearl could come up with. 'And he's told me all about his first wife and why the marriage collapsed. It seems to have ended much more amicably than mine.' She made an effort to smile. 'At least they're both still friends. Can't you at least give him a chance?'

Pearl sighed. Her eyes fell on the photo propped on her bedside table – a recent one of her and her mum, arms round each other, faces smiling at the camera. Mum often said they were best friends now, didn't she? And best friends should support each other. 'All right,' she said. 'We'll do the picnic. But please don't rush into things, Mum.'

Linda smiled at her and reached to squeeze her hand. 'Thanks, darling.'

A door banged downstairs. 'What time's dinner?' Harrison shouted. 'I'm starving.'

Linda gave a rueful laugh. 'Looks like I'd better get that lasagne out of the oven. And I need to tell Harrison about the picnic on Sunday too. Will you come down with me for moral support?'

'Of course.' Pearl got off the bed, feeling slightly stiff after the day's exertions. She followed her mum downstairs, wondering if she was making a mountain out of a molehill. Maybe Edward would turn out to be perfectly nice and exactly the sort of person it would be nice to know? And what about his son? Linda hadn't said what he was called, or told her anything about him. Pearl pictured a tall, fit boy, into athletics like his dad . . . Maybe they'd have something in common?

Well, there was no getting out of this picnic now, however she felt. Unless there was a sudden downpour, of course.

♥

That evening, Pearl nearly didn't bother to log on to her netbook. Her stomach felt unpleasantly full from the enormous helping of lasagne her mother had absent-mindedly ladled onto her plate. Harrison had been in a good mood for once, and Linda had spent most of the meal asking him questions about his music and being nice to him. Then, at the end, she'd casually mentioned the picnic on Sunday.

'I'm out on Sunday,' Harrison said instantly.

Linda's face fell. 'Can't you rearrange?'

He shrugged. 'Sorry, I'm busy.'

'Revising?'

'Yeah.' But Harrison looked shifty, and Pearl guessed he wouldn't be revising at all. In fact, she suspected he hadn't any plans for Sunday at all but simply made up an excuse to avoid the picnic. She felt cross with him for spoiling things. Mum didn't ask much of him, did she? So why couldn't he see how much this meant to her?

She lay down on the bed, but her stomach gurgled so much she couldn't get to sleep, so she sat up and switched on the netbook instead.

There were no new emails. But as she stared at the screen and wondered whether she could be bothered to check the British Synchro site for any news, a window popped up. 'Chat to Bailey?' it asked. Pearl's eyebrows rose. Chat to Bailey? Did she want to? Then she shrugged and hit 'Yes'. After all, there was nothing else to do.

Bailey: Hi, Pearl. U OK?

Pearl: Hi. I'm OK, u?

Bailey: Not 2 bad. Cud b better.

Pearl: ?

Bailey: School.

Pearl: Oh. Sorry. U want 2 tlk about it?

Bailey: No, it makes me sound like a whinger. I hate being taught stuff that's pointless, that's all. Wish I didn't have to go. UR so lucky!

Pearl: I guess. Tho sometimes I wish I did – feel I miss out on normal stuff.

Bailey: UR not missing anything, I promise u! How's the swimming?

Pearl: Grim. Got Spanish coach atm and every1 hates her.

Bailey: Y?

Pearl: She picks on us, criticizes EVERYTHING, made Evie cry 2day.

Bailey: That's really bad, have u told yr boss?

Pearl: Yes. We went 2c her 2day and told her we'll all walk out if she doesn't fire the Spanish woman!!!!

Bailey: That's mental! Can u do that?

Pearl: Not done it b4, no idea what'll happen!

Bailey: Sounds like we both had a bad day.
Pearl: Yeah. And y is it that when I bad thing happens, along comes another?
Bailey: ?

Pearl hesitated. Should she tell him? But before she could stop herself, she had typed:

Pearl: Oh it's not really bad. Am probably being OTT.
Bailey: About what?
Pearl: Mum has new boyf. Feel weird about it.
Bailey: Oh. U don't like him?
Pearl: No. Maybe. I just think it's 2 soon.
Bailey: Soon after what?
Pearl: Dad left 7 months ago.
Bailey: Oh. R they getting divorced?
Pearl: Yeah.
Bailey: Mine are divorced 2.
Pearl: Really?? When?
Bailey: Couple of years. It was OK really. Better afterwards. And u get 2 loads of presents at xmas!!
Pearl: LOL. I don't think I want presents from my dad ever again.
Bailey: Oh dear, that bad?
Pearl: He keeps trying 2 talk to me but I don't want 2. U know when he walked out? It was the day I was

picked 4 the Olympic team. I got home and he was
gone. Can you believe it?

Bailey: That's horrible. No wonder ur so mad at him.

Pearl: I don't think I can ever forgive him.

Bailey: U might. It gets better over time. And there
might have been stuff going on that u didn't know
about.

Pearl: Like what?

Bailey: I dunno. But maybe a reason why it was that
day, that time.

Pearl: I don't think there would be a good enough
reason.

Bailey: How do you know if u don't talk to him?

Pearl: What is this?? Why are you telling me what to
do?? I don't want 2 talk to him, OK!!!

Bailey: Sorry.

Pearl sat back and took a breath. She really
wanted to log off now. This had been a bad idea,
talking to Bailey. She hardly knew him, did she?
And here he was, telling her what to do about her
dad!

A new message flashed up on screen.

Bailey: REALLY sorry. None of my business. I was
mad at both my parents when they split up, but

things got better and now Mum's getting married again. Her new man is really nice.

It was almost as though Bailey thought that by typing very quickly, he might prevent Pearl from logging off. She found herself reading his words, mesmerized; her finger hovering over the 'disconnect' button.

Bailey: Looking back, I think I was more scared than angry. I thought I'd get forgotten when they started new lives, and I hated telling people my parents had split. It made us sound like a family failure or something stupid like that. But Mum's so happy now, it was obviously the right thing to do. And Dad goes out with people too, tho he hasn't really found the right person yet. He's started seeing a new woman but I don't think she's right for him either.

Pearl couldn't resist.

Pearl: Y not?
Bailey: He says she's really nice and sweet and all that but she texts him ALL the time! Like evry HOUR it's ridiculous! They've hardly been out or anything yet!

Pearl: OMG, creepy! How do u know, did your dad tell you?

Bailey: His phone's always beeping and it's always her. He smiles when he gets the texts but he did say yesterday how she keeps asking questions.

Pearl: That does sound weird, maybe your dad should steer clear of her.

Bailey: I did say she sounded like The Neediest Woman In The World but he just laughed at me.

Pearl: LOL!

Bailey: Oh well, I guess he can look after himself. Just don't want 2c him taken 4 a ride, that's all.

Pearl: That's JUST how I feel about my mum. I don't want her to get hurt again ☹

Bailey: It's hard not 2 worry. Sometimes it feels like we're the parents!

Pearl: Exactly!

Bailey: I gotta go now, sorry. Good to talk tho.

Pearl: Really nice 2 talk 2 u too.

And she meant it. It had been nice to share her feelings with someone who understood what she was going through – and somehow, typing it into the computer made it less scary. Pearl was surprised how much she had told Bailey about her feelings. When you weren't face-to-face, it was easier to find the words.

> Bailey: Talk again soon?
> Pearl: Yeah, will prob need 2 Sunday evening!!
> Bailey: What's happening Sunday?
> Pearl: Never mind, tell you then!
> Bailey: K.
> Pearl: Thanks Bailey.
> Bailey: Ur welcome. Cu l8r!

He signed off. Pearl sat back and smiled. Bailey did have a way of making her feel better. She laughed out loud as she thought about his dad's new girlfriend – she sounded like a right horror! Glancing at the clock, she was astonished to see the time – over an hour had gone by and she hadn't even realized!

Snuggling down under the duvet, she wished she'd asked Bailey's advice about how to deal with the picnic on Sunday afternoon. He might have had some good ideas. But maybe the girls would be able to help when she saw them in the morning.

Chapter 8

nothing like a blind date!

'We're taking you for a makeover,' said Evie firmly, as soon as Pearl arrived at the shopping centre on Sunday.

Pearl laughed. 'Why?'

'So that you can look beautiful when you meet Edward's son, of course,' Evie explained. Millie grinned.

'You guys are mad,' said Pearl, amused. 'He might be horrible!'

'Or he might be gorgeous,' countered Evie.

Millie tugged on Pearl's arm. 'Better just agree,' she advised. 'She's made up her mind anyway!'

'Oh, all right.' Pearl allowed the other two to drag her into a department store. 'But no weird eye shadow or red lipstick. I get enough over-the-top makeup when we're doing a competition.'

'Of course not,' said Evie, looking horrified. 'Subtle but enhancing, that's what we're going for.'

'She read that in a magazine,' whispered Millie, and Pearl giggled.

It took a while for Evie to decide which brand would be best and she was deaf to any suggestions from the other two. 'Bobbi Brown,' she said in the end, nodding. 'Because it's funky but natural and they have a great range of foundations.'

Pearl rolled her eyes at Millie, who burst out laughing.

'You're not taking this seriously!' complained Evie.

'Sorry.' Pearl tried to compose herself.

'Can I help you?' asked the assistant.

'My friend here would like a makeover,' said Evie, pulling Pearl forward. 'If that's possible.'

'Of course!' The girl smiled brightly. 'I'd love to – and we have some great colours that would really suit you. Have a seat.'

'Thanks.' Pearl sat down on a tall stool next to the display. 'I don't want much; it's not for a party or anything.'

'Natural daywear,' said the girl, nodding her head. 'I get it. What's your name?'

'Pearl.'

'Gorgeous name. I'm Naiha.'

'Hi.'

'I was going to ask if you could take off any makeup, but you're not wearing any, are you?' Naiha gazed critically at Pearl's face.

'No. I don't usually bother.'

'Really?' Naiha busied herself collecting bottles and jars and pots from the counter. 'I can't leave the house without doing my face. Makes me feel more confident, you know?'

'Right.' Pearl glanced at Naiha's face. It was indeed carefully made up, with sweeping liner both above and below her eyes, and a subtle shimmer on her cheeks. 'I – ah – I don't think I need quite as much as that.'

'Go for it,' Evie broke in, ignoring Pearl. She grinned at Naiha. 'Pearl might be meeting a very important boy this afternoon.'

'Really?' Naiha's plucked eyebrows rose into her forehead. 'Who's this then?' She began wiping Pearl's face with a cotton pad soaked in cleanser.

'He's nobody,' said Pearl, wishing her friends weren't watching so closely. 'They're being silly.'

'Her mum has started seeing a new bloke,' Evie told Naiha, 'and he's got a son. Pearl's going to meet him for the first time today.'

'I see,' said Naiha. 'Like a blind date.'

'No!' cried Pearl. 'Nothing like a blind date!'

'Try to keep still,' Naiha told her. She began sweeping foundation across Pearl's cheekbones with a brush.

'You have to think positive,' Evie told Pearl. 'He could be the perfect boy to date. If his dad and your mum are going out . . .'

'You are . . .' Pearl ran out of words. 'This is ridiculous. Only a couple of weeks ago you were telling me to go out with Bailey!'

'You didn't though, did you?' argued Evie. 'So now we're back to square one.'

'I talked to him on Friday night,' said Pearl, and immediately wanted to take back the words.

Evie took a step closer, and Millie gave a small gasp. 'You talked to Bailey? What, on the phone?'

'No, instant messenger,' said Pearl reluctantly.

'*And?*' asked Millie.

'And nothing!' said Pearl. 'We had a chat, that's all.'

'Sounds like you've got all the boys running after you,' commented Naiha, who was holding up various shades of eye shadow against Pearl's face and squinting at them.

'I haven't really,' said Pearl. 'Bailey's just a friend.' The word 'friend' felt funny to say. *Was* Bailey a friend? She supposed he must be, given the sort of chat they'd had. She wouldn't talk like that to someone who wasn't a friend, would she?

'You're so lucky,' said Millie, somewhat enviously. 'I wish I had a boy to chat to on IM. But there's only my brother's stupid friends and they're all younger than me, and so immature.'

'Older boys are definitely better,' said Naiha, finding a tiny brush and starting on Pearl's eyelids. 'I used to go out with this boy my age, but I dumped him when I realized he was only interested in himself. Now I've met someone older. He's a drama student.'

'That sounds cool,' said Millie, impressed.

'I want to be an actress,' confided Naiha. 'My dad's a film director in Bollywood and when I leave school I'm going out there to work.'

'Wow!' Evie looked at Naiha with respect. 'I used to think I wanted to act. Shame I don't really have time now.'

'There's always time for drama club,' Naiha told her.

'Not for us.' Evie shook her head regretfully. 'Our training schedule is too tight.'

'Training schedule?' Naiha was puzzled. 'What do you mean?'

Pearl hesitated. 'We're swimmers. We're in a synchro team.'

Naiha looked blank. 'What's synchro?'

'Synchronized swimming,' explained Millie.

'Oh, right!' Naiha nodded. She dusted powder over Pearl's face before reaching for the eyeliner. 'What's that like, then?'

Pearl glanced at the other two. How did you explain synchro to someone who didn't know anything about it? 'It's hard work.'

'I guess you must train a lot of evenings,' said Naiha. 'To fit round school and everything.'

'N-no,' said Pearl reluctantly. 'I don't go to school. Not this year.'

Naiha stopped, looking astonished. 'What do you mean? Why not?'

'We're practising for the Olympics,' Evie said, seeing that Pearl wasn't sure what to say. 'You're not allowed to go to school in the year leading up to the Games. It's a British Swimming law thing.'

Naiha's wide, black-rimmed eyes flicked from one to the other. 'You're in the Olympics? Wow. That's like – wow.'

Pearl felt a rush of pride. It *was* wow, wasn't it? It didn't matter if people didn't know anything about synchro; you only had to say the magic words 'Olympic Games' and people immediately thought you were amazing.

'Seriously?' Naiha said. 'You're not having me on?'

Pearl smiled. 'No, we're not having you on.'

'Wow. Just wait till I tell my friends I met you.' Naiha was excited. 'Would you sign something for me? And I don't suppose I could get a photo, could I? On my phone?'

Pearl grinned. 'Of course. Maybe we'd better have your autograph too, so that when you're a famous actress we can say we knew you when you were working on the Bobbi Brown counter.'

Naiha pulled a face. 'It's just a weekend job for now. My mum's really stingy with my allowance. I've had worse jobs though.'

The four girls chatted and laughed until Naiha had finished making up Pearl's face, and then they took photos on Naiha's phone and signed some bits of paper for each other.

Pearl wasn't at all sure she liked what Naiha had done with her face. The mascara was so thickly applied that it made her feel like there were spiders just out of sight, and she could have done without the eyeliner entirely. As soon as they had left the department store (Pearl having purchased a powder compact so that

Naiha didn't feel all her work had been in vain), she turned to her friends. 'Seriously, do you like it?'

'I *do*,' said Evie honestly, 'but I'm not sure it's very *you*.'

'That's it,' said Pearl. 'I'm taking it off.'

'No, don't!' said Millie, and Evie agreed. 'It's more than you'd normally wear in the daytime, but you do look amazing. Your eyes look about twice as big, and that shimmer stuff she put on your cheeks is gorgeous.'

'Let's go and find some lunch,' suggested Evie, 'and then you can decide after that.'

As they walked towards the food hall, two different boys turned to look at Pearl. 'What did I tell you?' exclaimed Evie. 'I might go back to that girl and get her to do me too!'

Pearl felt embarrassed but pleased. Wearing makeup was a bit like wearing an outfit – you could almost pretend you were someone else. Maybe that would help when she met Edward's son?

❤

'You look lovely!' said her mum in a surprised voice when she picked up Pearl from the car park. 'Who did your makeup?'

'A girl at the Bobbi Brown counter,' Pearl told her. 'You don't think it's too much?'

'I think it's perfect.' Linda beamed at her. 'I'm so touched you're making the effort, darling. It means a lot to me.'

Pearl smiled back, but inside she felt nervous. It was half past three and the sun was still high in the sky, though there was a chilly breeze now. A picnic at this time of day might not be a success for reasons other than the people involved!

'Do *I* look all right?' her mother asked, anxiously patting her hair and trying to smooth down any wayward strands.

'You look great, Mum,' Pearl said. 'Honestly.'

They parked in a side street and Linda opened the boot so that they could take the food into the park. 'How many people are you feeding, Mum?' asked Pearl in dismay, staring at the six fully packed Tesco bags and two picnic blankets.

'I didn't know what everyone would like,' said her mum defensively. 'So I got lots. We can always put leftovers in the fridge.'

The two of them struggled, puffing and panting,

into the park and along a path. Pearl could feel herself getting hot and hoped her makeup would stay put and not slide down her face.

'Do you think this will do?' asked Linda, dumping her bags on a grassy spot. 'I can't carry these any further.'

They were on a slight slope overlooking the lake. Parchester Town Park had several really nice spots to meet, including a large grassy area surrounded by flowerbeds where the Circle Youth Theatre Company had performed their summer production for the past three years. Pearl had been to see *Romeo and Juliet* here and had enjoyed it very much, even though she wasn't all that keen on the theatre. There was also a wooded area with a so-called 'secret' garden, and a big lake frequented by ducks and geese. It was on the banks of this lake that Linda had arranged for them all to meet.

'It's not too windy,' said Pearl, looking up at the sky. 'It's just a shame it isn't a bit sunnier.'

'Do you think it's going to rain?' wondered Linda, following her gaze. 'Oh, I really hope not. That would spoil everything.'

'I'm sure it'll be fine,' said Pearl. 'Shall we get the stuff out?'

'I can't believe it's only a few hours since I last saw Edward,' said her mum, spreading out the picnic blanket. 'It feels like days.'

'Mmm.' Pearl had already heard about the date the previous night; Linda had been walking on air ever since. Pearl was pleased that her mum was happy but she still felt nervous about how fast everything seemed to be moving along. The way Linda was talking now – well, it was like she'd already decided that Edward was The One . . . and she hadn't known him long!

Pearl sighed, but then a thought struck her. At least her mother wasn't being texted every minute by her new boyfriend, in a creepy stalker-ish way! She must remember that Bailey's dad had it much worse! The thought made her smile.

'Oh!' Linda broke into her thoughts with a happy exclamation. 'He's here! There they are!' She pointed.

Two figures were making their way round the lake, carrying a large cool box and a couple of bags. Pearl squinted. They weren't very clear from here, but as they approached, she recognized Edward as the taller of the two. Edward was white, but his son was much darker . . . In fact he . . . Oh no . . . it couldn't be . . . That was impossible!

Pearl felt her stomach drop through the ground and she froze, unable to look away. The shorter of the two, walking beside his dad, getting closer and closer – was Bailey.

Chapter 9

I wish I could take back everything I said

'You!' Bailey looked as startled as she was.

Pearl was completely speechless. She couldn't tear her eyes away from him. Bailey – Bailey Ross – the boy she'd been pouring her heart out to . . . *he* was Edward's son! But how? 'What are you doing here?' she said stupidly.

'What are *you* doing here?'

'Edward's . . . your dad?'

'Yeah, of course.' Bailey's eyes flicked from Pearl to her mother. 'I didn't realize . . .' Speech deserted him for once. 'You look nice,' he added lamely.

Suddenly Pearl felt ridiculous in her new makeup.

Linda and Edward were bewildered. 'You know each other?' asked Edward.

'I interviewed Pearl for the magazine,' Bailey explained.

Edward's brow cleared. 'Ah! The synchronized swimmer – of course! What a coincidence!'

Linda smiled. 'This is brilliant! And you two didn't know? How amazing!'

Pearl tried to smile back, but all she could think of was the conversation with Bailey on Friday night and what he had said ... *The Neediest Woman In The World ... Don't want 2c him taken 4 a ride ...*

It had been her *mum* he was talking about! Her mum, who had been treated so badly by Dad, dumped after however many years of marriage, left to bring up her two kids on her own. The mum who had become Pearl's best friend. How could Bailey have called her such *horrible* things?

She felt bile rise in her throat. *I trusted you*, she thought. *I told you my innermost thoughts, my fears, my anxieties. And all the time you were slagging off my mum! How dare you!*

Bailey was looking uncomfortable too, as though he had also just remembered what he had said over the internet.

Linda hadn't noticed her daughter's expression and was chatting away happily. 'Well, I think it's *fate*! You and me, Edward, and we had no idea that our kids had already met!'

'Extraordinary,' he agreed. 'Like you say, almost as though it's meant to be.'

'I'm sorry Harrison couldn't come,' Linda said. 'He's revising for GCSEs, you know.'

Edward nodded. 'That's a lot of pressure.'

Linda seized on this gratefully. 'You're so right. He's become all moody and difficult. I have to remind myself that he's got a lot on his plate at the moment. Speaking of which . . . shall we get the food out?' She looked at the collection of bags and laughed. 'I think we'll have enough to feed everyone in the park!'

Edward grinned back. 'I told you I'd bring some as well. You didn't need to get this much.'

Linda looked at him with an expression Pearl hadn't seen on her face before. It was almost adoring. 'Don't they say the way to a man's heart is through his stomach?'

Pearl felt sick. Watching her mum flirt was so weird, like a friend telling you they fancy your brother. She didn't know where to look or what to say.

Linda reached out to Edward's face, and then seemed to remember they weren't the only ones there. She turned to Pearl. 'Listen, why don't you two go off and feed the ducks while we're getting the food out?' She dug a bread roll out of one of the bags. 'Come back in ten minutes.'

Edward smiled at Pearl. 'No rush,' he said.

Pearl clenched the roll in her hand, feeling the bread squash beneath its plastic wrapping. *They want us out of the way, so that they can . . . urgh.* Without looking at Bailey, she started down the bank towards the lake.

Once they were out of earshot, Bailey muttered, 'I'm so sorry, Pearl. I didn't know.'

'Shut up,' she said fiercely. 'Just shut up. I don't want to talk to you.'

'Pearl, I'd never have said those things if—'

'Shut *up*!' She whirled furiously to face him. 'I can't believe you were so – so *horrible*! I thought you were *nice*; I felt bad when you asked me out and I said no. I was even thinking it might be nice to see you again. But all that stuff – it was my *mum*, Bailey! How could you even say it?'

He looked down at the grass. 'I was trying to cheer you up. Maybe I went a bit far.'

'*Maybe?* Calling her the neediest woman in the world? You are such a – a . . .' Pearl couldn't think of a word bad enough.

'Well, she is needy,' retorted Bailey. 'She *has* been texting Dad every hour – she *does* keep hanging around the gym!'

'She hangs around the gym because she's waiting

for me, you moron! And of course she's texting him all the time – she can't stop thinking about him! Even though he's completely not worth it!'

'What are you talking about?' Bailey's expression darkened. 'There's nothing wrong with my dad!'

'Yeah? Then why is he divorced?' Pearl folded her arms. 'Why didn't your mum want him any more if he's so perfect?'

'Oh, come on! Your mum's getting divorced too, and at least my parents split up in a good way!'

'It wasn't Mum's fault! Dad was the one who walked out!'

'Yeah, but there are two people in a marriage, aren't there?' Bailey was angry now too. 'And maybe if she hadn't been so – so *needy*, he wouldn't have left her!'

Pearl stared at him, shocked. Tears pricked at her eyes. She felt so angry and hurt, she wanted to hit him.

Bailey realized he had gone too far. 'I'm sorry, I didn't mean to say that. It just came out. I didn't mean to say any of it, Pearl. I just – I guess I'm protective of my dad. I don't want him taken advantage of. But I don't know your mum and I made judgements. I'm sorry. I was wrong.'

'You totally were,' she whispered, afraid the tears were going to start flowing.

Bailey took an impulsive step towards her, but she flinched away. 'Pearl, I'm so sorry. I wish I could take back everything I said.'

'But you can't,' she said. *It's too late, he's said too much. And I thought we were becoming friends.* She wiped her eyes and realized she was still holding the bread roll. She tore open the plastic and upended the squashed contents onto the grass in a lump. Instantly, ducks came running from all directions, quacking loudly.

'We should get back to them,' said Bailey quietly. His arms hung by his sides. He looked defeated.

She nodded. 'But I'm not speaking to you again. Not like this, not online – never.'

'What about our parents?'

'I don't care. They can do what they like.'

They headed back up the slope in silence. Linda and Edward hadn't got very far with putting out the food and drink. They were lying on the blanket in an embrace. 'Hello,' said Bailey loudly.

They sprang apart. 'Hello, you're back!' said Edward. 'Goodness, is it ten minutes already?'

Pearl watched her mum trying to smooth down her rumpled top and felt sick again. 'Mum,' she said, 'I don't feel well.'

Linda looked up immediately, concerned. 'Really?'

She saw Pearl's red eyes and reached out. 'Come and sit down, love. What's the matter?'

Pearl shook her head. 'Just feel sick. Think I've got a temperature coming.' She hated lying to her mum, but the thought of eating a picnic with Edward and Bailey was more than she could bear. This was worse than anything she had imagined. To think her friends had persuaded her to have a makeover in order to impress the mystery boy!

Her mother bit her lip. 'Maybe eating something would make you feel better?'

'I only just had lunch.'

'Oh.' Linda cast a look at Edward, who immediately responded.

'You should take her home, Lin. She doesn't look well.' He glanced at Bailey. 'Did you two have a fight?'

Bailey hesitated. 'Sort of,' he said truthfully. 'It was something I said that I shouldn't.'

His father frowned. 'I hope you apologized.'

'I did. I have.'

'Well, then,' said Linda, not quite sure what to do. 'That's all right then, isn't it, Pearl?'

No it isn't. It isn't all right at all. Pearl felt trapped. Her mother had been so looking forward to this picnic! But how could she possibly pretend to be having a nice time? *Maybe if your mum hadn't been so needy, your dad wouldn't have left her* . . . The words played over and over in her head.

'Here you go – try this.' Linda unwrapped a smoked salmon sandwich and passed it to her. 'I'm sure once you've had a couple of mouthfuls you'll feel better.'

Pearl stared down at it. Fish and lemon dressing mingled in the air. She threw the sandwich onto the blanket, and just made it to the nearest flowerbed before she was sick.

♥

'No wonder you were so out of it this morning,' said Millie at lunch break the next day.

Evie and Hollie-Mae nodded. 'It was like you were on another planet,' said Evie. 'And you looked so pale. Well, you know what I mean. Ill.'

'And Mum was so cross with me for spoiling everything.' Pearl sighed. 'She went on and on about how I hadn't made an effort to get on with Bailey and how she'd wanted everything to be perfect when we all got together.'

'She should have known these things can't be planned,' said Hollie-Mae. 'My parents have both married other people and they don't get on at all!

After a while my dad stopped trying to make everyone happy and just accepted it.' She laughed. 'You can't just lump people together and expect them to get on.'

'*We* do,' said Millie, looking around the table and smiling at her friends.

'That's different. We're all mad about synchro. Gives us something in common.'

'So what happened when you got home?' asked Evie.

Pearl looked at her sandwiches. 'Mum told me if I was that sick I should go to bed. She had to throw half the picnic stuff away. She spent most of the evening on the phone to Edward. Probably moaning about me.'

'You don't know that,' said Millie comfortingly. 'Besides, she adores you.'

'Not any more. Not now she's got *Edward*.'

'What about your brother – what did he say?' asked Evie.

'He didn't come home till eight o'clock. I heard Mum having a go at him. I haven't talked to him.'

'I think it was really horrible of Bailey to say all that stuff over IM,' said Hollie-Mae.

'He didn't know it was Pearl's mum he was talking about,' argued Evie.

'That just makes it worse. He was being really nasty

about someone he didn't even know. And then he did say that thing about how Pearl's dad wouldn't have left if her mum wasn't needy. Right to Pearl's face!'

'Oh, let's not talk about it any more,' said Pearl miserably. 'It just makes me feel sick again.'

'Group hug,' said Evie, and the other three leaned over the table to link arms around each other's shoulders. 'At least we didn't have Carolina this morning.'

'Maybe she's left?' said Millie hopefully.

'Fingers crossed,' agreed Evie with a grin. 'Maybe everyone's pretending she never existed and we'll never hear about her again.'

But as they filed into the gym for their afternoon session, the girls were surprised to see their team manager, Emily, waiting for them. 'I won't beat around the bush,' she said sternly. The girls exchanged nervous glances. 'Carolina has gone back to Spain,' she went on, ignoring the murmurs that broke out at this. 'We had words over the weekend and we both felt it would be better for her to cut her visit short. I do not wish to discuss this again with you, but I would like to say one thing. Storming into my office and threatening to boycott practices is unacceptable behaviour. You are privileged young women. You have responsibilities. You have sponsors. A lot of people have put time, effort and money into training you and making you ready for the Olympics, and I do not appreciate being blackmailed into decisions. Anyone – and I mean *anyone* – who tries to pull that kind of stunt again will be thrown off the team, no second chances. Do I make myself clear?'

Pearl nodded fervently, her heart thumping. Emily was so rarely angry that it was a scary sight. She could see the other eight girls nodding and muttering 'Yes' too.

'Good. There's an end of it,' said Emily. 'And I don't want to hear one word about Carolina from any of you, either to me or to each other. That chapter is closed. Bonnie will be taking your practices as usual.' She went out.

There was a collective exhaling of breath, and then excited chatter broke out. 'She's gone, she's gone!' cried Georgie, seizing Primrose's hands and swinging her round in a silly dance. 'Rejoice, rejoice!'

'Sssh!' said Jen in alarm. 'Didn't you hear what Emily just said? We can't talk about her at all.'

'Did I mention her name?' asked Georgie, her eyebrows raised and her eyes sparkling. 'Did I even mention her nationality? I could have been talking about anyone!' She let out a giggle. 'Bet you're pleased, Evie!'

Evie was shaking her head in disbelief. 'I can't take it in. She must be joking. I thought my life was going to be hell for the next couple of weeks.'

'Well, it won't be! We're freeeeee!' Georgie zoomed around the gym with her arms outstretched.

'What's going on?'

Georgie froze mid-flight as a man pushed the door open and stood there frowning. Pearl gulped and edged behind Kat. It was Edward.

'Are you girls supposed to be training in here?' he asked, his eyebrows drawn together.

'Yes,' said Jen. 'Sorry. Steve's not here yet.'

'He's been delayed,' Edward said. 'They just had a call from him at the front desk. Can you start without him?'

'Yes.' The girls nodded. 'Sorry again,' added Jen. 'We just had some good news.'

Edward smiled at her. 'Always nice to get good news on a Monday.'

The door banged behind him.

'He is *cute*!' said Lizzie admiringly.

Millie turned to Pearl. 'That's Edward though, isn't it?'

Pearl nodded, her lips pressed tightly together.

'Seriously?' asked Lizzie. 'The one your mum's dating? She's scooped a hottie there!'

Millie frowned at her, trying to send silent signals. 'Pearl's not happy about it.'

'Oh.' Lizzie saw Pearl's expression. 'Sorry. Uh – I'm sure looks can be deceiving.'

Yes, thought Pearl, her thoughts boomeranging to Bailey. *They certainly can.*

Chapter 10

this place is gorgeous

'You've been working so hard recently,' Emily told them one morning, 'that we all feel you deserve a treat.'

The girls exchanged curious glances. Training had certainly intensified over the past couple of weeks, and Pearl now found herself unable to stay awake past nine p.m., she was so tired. In some ways, this was a good thing, because her mum was still seeing Edward (though she had thankfully not suggested bringing the two families together again) and it meant that Pearl didn't have to think about this much. Bailey had emailed five times since the picnic, apologizing again and again, but Pearl couldn't bring herself to write back. What could she say?

'Training is about to step up another notch,' Emily went on, and Pearl dragged herself back to the present, 'and of course it's only two weeks now before we move

into the Athletes' Village, so before we take away all
your spare time, I've arranged for you to spend a day
in the spa at the Kellerman Club.'

Kat and Lizzie let out excited squeaks. 'We love that
place!' Pearl, Millie and Evie beamed at each other. A
treat indeed!

The Kellerman Club in Parchester was an exclusive
sports and leisure centre that charged very high
membership fees. It also had a large spa which offered
health and beauty treatments alongside jacuzzis and
saunas. There were Kellerman Clubs in thirteen cities
and towns across the country now, and two years ago
the chain had agreed to contribute to the sponsorship
of the British Synchro team.

'You'll each be able to have a couple of treatments,'
Emily said, smiling at the reaction. 'I've got some
lists, so you can choose. They do all sorts, from hot
stones to aromatherapy and flotation tanks – though
I'm guessing,' she added, amused, 'that you might
not want to spend your time floating in yet more
water.'

'When are we going?' asked Georgie eagerly.

'Thursday,' replied Emily. 'So you've got two more
days of really hard work before we take you into
Parchester by coach. Bring all your Team GB stuff too;
they'd like a photo of you all in the club, which is the

least we can do, seeing as you're getting a whole day of fun for nothing.' She grinned. 'And if Bonnie tells me you've slacked off in the next forty-eight hours, I can always cancel the Kellerman day for more training.'

The girls' mouths dropped open in horror and Emily laughed.

'We'll work twice as hard,' said Georgie in determination. 'A whole day at a spa! I can't believe it!'

Pearl thought of it in delight. Her entire body was full of little aches and pains and twinges. A day at a spa would be a dream come true!

♥

'Makes our centre look a bit shabby, doesn't it?' Millie whispered to Pearl as they stepped onto the luxurious carpet of the Kellerman Club foyer.

Pearl nodded. 'Totally. I mean, we've got up-to-date equipment and all that, but this place – wow. Look at the chairs!'

'I love the drapes,' added Millie, looking up at the great swathes of blue chiffon that hung from the ceiling. 'Kind of underwatery.'

'We haven't come to swim,' Pearl told her with a smile. 'We've come to be *pampered*.'

Millie giggled. 'I know. I can't believe it. I've never even had my nails done before, have you?'

'No. The closest I've come is that makeover you guys took me for in the shopping centre. I didn't know what to choose from the list of treatments here, so I went for a facial. I hope it's nice.'

'In a place like this?' Millie waved an arm. 'Bound to be. Can you imagine what we'd be paying for a day here normally?'

'Good thing they're sponsoring the team, then,' interrupted Evie, overhearing. Her eyes sparkled. 'I want a hot stone massage, an aromatherapy facial, reflexology and a relaxation session.'

Pearl laughed. 'You're supposed to choose two!'

'I'm hoping they'll bend the rules,' said Evie. 'Besides, the relaxation session isn't a treatment; it's a room you just go into and relax in.'

'This way!' called Jen, waving from the reception desk. 'Through to the changing rooms!'

The rest of the synchro team followed, casting admiring glances around as they went. 'I could *live* here,' declared Millie.

Pearl felt the same way. They had been to nice clubs and centres to train before, of course – sometimes the facilities abroad were amazing – but this place had a lovely atmosphere. There was a faint scent of lilies in the air, and the lighting was so subtle you couldn't even see where it was coming from. A woman in a white and blue uniform was leading the way down a wooden-panelled corridor to a white door at the end. The whole place felt calm and peaceful, rather than the streamlined, focused, high performance environment Pearl was used to.

Millie was practically euphoric about the changing rooms. 'Have you *seen* this?' she yelped, pulling a long white bathrobe out of her locker. 'These cost about thirty quid in Marks and Spencer's! Omigosh, and flip-flops too! And an eye mask! I am *so* saving up for a subscription to this place.'

'You'd have to save up for a long time,' Georgie advised her, tying her frizzy red hair back with a white band. 'I've seen the prices.'

'Remember we all have to put on the GB swimming costumes to start with,' Jen called over. 'They want a photo in the lounge area, by the fishpond.'

'Fishpond?' Millie pretended to faint. 'This is all too much.'

Pearl laughed. 'Come on. Otherwise we'll be late for all that relaxing.'

The nine girls, attired in their white bathrobes and Team GB swimming costumes, filtered out of the changing room and into a large open area bordered with padded mattresses and comfy cushions. In the middle was a large sunken pond, in which koi carp could be seen swimming lazily. Pearl felt her heart beat excitedly. How many girls her age had the chance to come to a place like this? Synchro might be hard work, but it did have its benefits!

There was a photographer setting up a camera, and several other people, including a friendly-looking tanned man in his fifties accompanied by a tall blonde teenage girl. Pearl smiled shyly at her as their gazes met, and the girl immediately beamed back and came over. 'Hi there,' she said. 'Have you got everything you need?'

'Yes thanks,' said Pearl, wondering who she was. She wasn't wearing a uniform like the other staff. 'This place is gorgeous. My friend Millie wants to live here.'

The blonde girl giggled. 'Thanks. My stepdad will be pleased.'

'Your stepdad?' Pearl glanced over at the man, who was chatting to the photographer.

'Corin Kellerman, the owner,' replied the girl. 'I'm Lola. I shouldn't really be here, but I begged him to let me come. I think what you guys do is amazing!'

'Oh – thanks.' Pearl was a little surprised. 'Not

many people know much about synchro. It's always nice to hear someone enjoys it.'

'Are you kidding? It's fantastic! I had a go once – me and my sister went on a one-day course thing. She was pretty good, actually, but I couldn't get the hang of being upside-down so much.' Lola pulled a face. 'I had no idea how hard it was until we tried it.'

'That's what everyone says,' agreed Pearl. 'People think it's just floating around, making nice patterns.'

'Well, I think you're all brilliant,' Lola told her. 'And I'm so excited you're going to spend the day here. You must check out the new hot mud treatment; it's completely blissful. And make sure you get Amelia if you're having a facial; she's the best.'

'What's this?' Millie came to join them. 'Are you getting tips, Pearl?'

'This is Millie,' Pearl said to Lola. 'She's the one who wants to live here.'

'I totally do!' exclaimed Millie. 'Everything here – I mean, you've got it all. It's like my idea of heaven. All these cushions to lie down on, and people to bring you drinks and new bathrobes – I *adore* the bathrobes – and even the stuff out in reception, all those beautiful drapes and things . . .' She sighed.

Lola blushed. 'You really like the drapes? They were my idea.'

'Really?' Millie stared at her. 'They're so pretty, like waves.'

'That's exactly the look I was going for.' Lola beamed. 'You see, Corin got this design firm in to do all the décor, but he hated everything they did, so he fired them. And then he let me have a go, and he liked my ideas miles better, so I basically did it all. The cushions, the drapes, the candles, the fragrance – all of it.'

'Wow.' Millie and Pearl looked at her with respect. 'That's really clever.'

Lola went even pinker, but she was saved from replying by a call from the photographer.

'Can I have everyone over here, sitting on this mat, please?'

'Talk to you later,' Lola said. 'And ask me if there's anything you want to know.' She beamed again. 'It's so exciting to meet real Olympic swimmers!'

The photo call didn't take long, and then they were allowed to start the serious business of relaxing. Pearl's facial wasn't for another half an hour, so she and Millie went to sit in the relaxation room, which was in semi-darkness and had super-comfy reclining chairs. Soft music played very quietly in the background, and a discreet assistant brought them glasses of peppermint cordial. 'Can you believe people come here every week?' Pearl said in wonder.

'When I'm rich,' said Millie, 'I shall come here every *day*.'

Pearl settled herself back into her chair and smiled. 'How are you going to get rich, Millie?'

'Writing books,' said Millie simply. 'When I've retired from synchro, I'll have my books published.'

Pearl turned her head to look at her curiously. 'Have you already written one, then?'

Millie blushed in the darkness. 'Three, actually. I'm not saying they're any good,' she added hastily. 'They might be rubbish. But if I keep going, then I'll get better, right? And then I can go straight from one career to another.'

'Can I read one?' asked Pearl.

She could hear her friend hesitate. 'Would you hate me if I said no?' replied Millie frankly. 'I haven't shown them to anyone. They're just for me for the moment.'

'What are they about?' asked Pearl, intrigued. She knew Millie loved reading; she always had her nose in a book. Cathy Cassidy, Hilary McKay, Jo Nadin, Jane Austen, Charlotte Brontë . . . Millie read anything and everything she could get her hands on, borrowing armfuls from the library every week.

But Pearl had never imagined that her friend wrote stories too.

'All sorts of things,' said Millie, sounding more enthusiastic. 'The one I'm writing at the moment is about this girl whose parents suddenly disappear while they're in the Amazon, and she has to go out there to look for them.'

'Why were they on holiday without her?' asked Pearl.

'They're on an expedition,' said Millie. 'They're out in the Amazon to see what damage is being done to the trees and all that. And it turns out they've been kidnapped because they've found some vital evidence that proves the government has been secretly cutting down the rainforest.'

'Which government?' asked Pearl.

'The British one.'

'Why would they be cutting down the rainforest?' Pearl was confused.

'Because they're the *government*,' said Millie, as though that explained everything. 'Anyway, the daughter has to go out there and hunt for them, and she nearly gets kidnapped herself, and then she meets this boy who lives with a tribe but he isn't one of them; he's got these magic powers . . .'

Pearl sat back and listened. It all sounded very

exciting – and wildly improbable, but she didn't dare say so. Besides, Millie read loads more books than she did, so presumably Millie knew how to write stories too.

'And then somehow she gets out of the security compound,' went on Millie. 'I haven't quite worked that bit out yet. And she tricks the guards so she can rescue her parents, and then they escape through a series of underground tunnels that the boy tells her about.'

'Wow,' said Pearl. 'It sounds amazing.'

'Thanks.' Millie was pleased. 'I'm thinking that if I keep all my stories in a drawer or on a computer or something, then in another ten years or so, I can retire from synchro and start earning loads of money from my books. Because I'll have built up a good store, you know, and they can publish lots at once.'

'Do you love writing more than synchro?' Pearl asked.

'Hmm.' Millie considered. 'I do love synchro, but there's something about writing . . . Maybe it's because I can do it on my own, and it's like going into my imagination and seeing what's there – that's exciting. And every time it's different. I mean, when we swim, we always do the same kinds of things. The same routines, the same moves – just in a different order.'

'You could say the same thing about writing,' pointed out Pearl, pleased with her own observation. 'The same words, just putting them in a different order.'

Millie laughed. 'Yeah, I guess so. But I'm the one making up the order. I don't know. Haven't you got something you're dying to do after you finish synchro?'

'No, I don't think so.' Pearl stared at the ceiling. 'I mean, I hadn't really thought beyond synchro, to be honest. I know it won't go on for ever, but I can't imagine doing anything else. Maybe I could be a coach or something. Do what Bonnie does.'

A woman had just come into the relaxation room, clutching her eye mask and a magazine. She glared at the two girls and said, 'Shhh.'

Pearl caught Millie's eye and the two of them tried not to giggle. 'Ten minutes before I have to go off for my facial,' whispered Pearl. 'We'd better get in some proper relaxation.'

Millie nodded, her expression still amused.

They sat back and Pearl closed her eyes. Had she ever felt so comfortable before? She didn't think so. Where did they get these amazing chairs?

And that music playing – it was so soothing, washing over you.

She must not fall asleep. She only had ten minutes before she had to go and have her facial . . .

♥

'That was the best day ever,' said Evie, sighing dramatically. The girls were in the changing rooms again, getting ready to go home.

Millie looked almost tearful. 'I can't believe it's gone so fast. I want to stay here. Do you think we could suggest to Emily that we need to come every month?'

Pearl gave her friend a sympathetic hug. 'That would be amazing, wouldn't it? I feel different too – sort of lighter. And nothing hurts the way it did yesterday. The skin on my face feels gorgeous.' She yawned. 'But I feel as if I could sleep for a week!'

Gradually, with much reluctance, the girls got ready to face the outside world again. 'Training tomorrow,' groaned Georgie.

Pearl took a last look back at the changing room, with its wooden lockers, hand cream, cotton wool and kindly-lit mirrors. 'But we've had today,' she said wistfully. 'We can always look back on it.'

'I might cry if I do that,' muttered Millie. 'It was so perfect!'

Pearl thought of Lola, the girl she'd met that morning who had done all the décor for her stepdad. Lola would love to hear how much the girls had enjoyed it. 'You go on,' she said suddenly as they headed through the foyer. 'I just want to have a quick word with someone.' Millie and Evie looked puzzled. 'To say how much we enjoyed it,' Pearl explained. 'You know . . .'

The other two nodded. 'We'll see you tomorrow,' said Evie, her eyes sliding across to the doorway. 'Blast, there goes my bus.'

'I expect my mum's in the car park,' said Millie. 'See you tomorrow, Pearl.'

'Yup, see you.' Pearl went up to the reception desk.

The uniformed girl behind it looked up and smiled. 'Hello there, can I help you?'

'Is – is Lola here?' asked Pearl. 'I mean, it doesn't matter if she isn't, but I saw her this morning . . .'

'Lola Cassidy?' asked the receptionist. 'You mean – Oh yes, she was here this morning, wasn't she? No, I'm afraid she went back to school.'

'Oh,' said Pearl, suddenly feeling foolish. Of course Lola had gone to school! That's where girls her age were during normal weekdays!

'Did you want to leave her a note?' asked the

receptionist. A door to the side opened, and the friendly-looking man Pearl had seen that morning came out. 'Oh, here's Mr Kellerman,' said the girl. 'He can pass on a message to Lola.'

'What's that?' Corin Kellerman came over, smiling. 'Are you a friend of Lola's?'

'No.' Pearl almost wished she hadn't started this now – only she did want to thank everyone for such a lovely day. 'No, it's just that I met her this morning and she was telling me about the décor and how she designed it . . .'

'That's right.' Corin beamed. 'Did a fantastic job too, didn't she?'

'Yes.' Pearl smiled back. 'That's sort of what I wanted to tell her. Me and my friends, we just loved everything about today. We wanted to thank you for letting us come.'

'You're most welcome,' said Corin. 'From what I hear, you girls work very hard. Everyone deserves a bit of time off.'

'Well, it was brilliant,' said Pearl. 'And please tell Lola we loved the way it looks too. My friend Millie was practically crying as she left; she didn't want to go home!'

Corin laughed. 'That's the best reaction I've heard. What was your name?'

'Pearl. Pearl Okeke.'

'Well, it was very nice to meet you, Pearl.' Corin held out a hand, just as a woman came into the foyer, clutching a large black leather bag and looking flustered.

'You too.'

'Have I missed them?' panted the woman to the receptionist.

The girl behind the desk looked confused. 'Missed who, madam?'

'The swimmers. Have they gone?'

'Oh – um . . .' The receptionist glanced at Pearl, and the woman with the bag saw the look. Instantly, a smile spread across her face. She was wearing bright pink lipstick that was slightly smudged at one corner.

'Hello,' she said, holding out a hand. 'It's so lovely to meet you. I was afraid I was too late.' Pearl had no option but to shake her hand.

Corin stepped forward. 'Hi there,' he said breezily, also holding out a hand. 'Corin Kellerman. This is my club. And you are . . . ?'

'Melissa Troughton,' said the woman, shaking his hand vigorously. '*Daily Post*. I was hoping to get a few words from one of the girls for an article I'm writing.'

'I see.' Corin nodded. Then he turned to Pearl.

'What do you think, Pearl, is that all right with you?'

Pearl hesitated.

'I won't be long,' said Melissa Troughton pleadingly. 'Only I got caught up in this event earlier today, and the traffic on the way here was murder . . .'

Pearl wasn't sure what to do. Normally interviews were arranged by Emily. Should she speak to a journalist without checking it was all right? But if it was just a few words, like the lady said . . . 'All right,' she said. 'But my mum's picking me up any minute.'

Melissa beamed, showing very white teeth between the pink lips. 'Thanks so much, sweetheart. Is there a quiet spot we could go?' she asked Corin.

'You can use my office.'

With the door shut, Pearl suddenly felt even more nervous about being in the room with the journalist. But Melissa seemed very friendly, poking around in her bag for her digital recorder and accidentally spilling tissues and car keys onto the floor. 'Sorry, sorry,' she said, her blonde curly hair escaping in wisps from its clip. 'Be with you in just a sec . . . Here we are!' She clicked on the recorder. 'Thanks so much for agreeing to talk to me. Now, what's your name?'

'Pearl Okeke.'

'How do you spell your surname? Just so that I get it right in the article.'

Pearl spelled it for her. Melissa smiled. 'Thanks. So you and the rest of the British Synchro team have been here for the day – is that right?'

'Yes.' Pearl felt on surer ground here. 'It's been lovely.'

'I bet. Do you come to this kind of place a lot?'

Pearl laughed. 'No, never. We don't really have time – and of course it's very expensive here.' Should she have said that? Did it sound like she was complaining she didn't have enough money?

But Melissa was picking up on her other point. 'Of course, you spend a lot of time training, don't you? How many hours a week, would you say?'

'Um . . .' Pearl tried to think. 'I don't really know. Maybe . . . uh . . . forty?'

'Forty hours, really! Goodness. And you don't go to school, is that right?'

'Yes.' Once again, Pearl explained the rules.

Melissa nodded. 'You must have been very excited to be chosen for the team. Are you the youngest? You're what – fifteen?'

'Fourteen. And yes, I'm the youngest, but only by a year.'

'A great honour to represent your country at the Olympics at your age,' suggested Melissa.

'Yes, it is.'

146

'And where are you from, originally?'

Pearl was puzzled. 'Parchester.'

'Yes, but before that?'

'I don't know what you mean. I was born in Parchester. I've never lived anywhere else.'

Melissa laughed. 'Sorry, I don't mean to confuse you. Where's your family from? That's what I mean.'

'Er . . . Dad was from Birmingham . . .'

'No, no, which country? Kenya? Zimbabwe?'

Pearl stared. 'He's British. We're all British. I mean, my grandparents lived in Nigeria for a while, I think . . .'

'Nigeria,' Melissa said, nodding. 'Right. That's great. And how do you feel, with your Nigerian heritage, about representing Great Britain?'

Pearl was totally baffled now. Nigerian heritage? She'd never felt like she had any! 'Um . . . do you mean I should be representing Nigeria?' she asked hesitantly.

'No, not at all!' Melissa laughed again. *Does she ever look unhappy?* Pearl wondered. 'But do you feel especially proud that you're a symbol of multicultural Britain in international sport?'

'A symbol? Me?'

'Well, of course! Look at what you've achieved – a black member of the British Olympic Synchro team!

It's such a white sport, isn't it? You must feel proud.'

'Er . . .' said Pearl, starting to fidget on her chair. This conversation was starting to go in a direction that made her uncomfortable. 'Yeah, I guess so. Look, I really should be going . . .'

'It was lovely talking to you,' said Melissa, her smile stretching so wide it practically reached her ears. She snapped off the recorder and shook Pearl's hand again. 'Thanks so much for sparing me a few minutes, Pearl. Best of luck in the competition!'

'Thanks.' Pearl made her escape.

Chapter 11

a black Pearl in the British oyster

Pearl, on the running machine, was surprised to see Emily coming into the gym the following Monday. She was holding a newspaper, and her face was stern. 'Pearl,' she called. 'I need a word with you, please.'

Pearl felt cold. What had she done? She glanced at Millie, who shrugged, equally baffled. She stepped off the machine and followed Emily out into reception.

It was quiet at this time of the morning, but Emily didn't stop to sit down. Instead, she took Pearl all the way to her office. Now Pearl was really alarmed. What could be so bad she couldn't discuss it in public?

'Have you seen this?' Emily held up the newspaper. It was today's *Daily Post*.

Pearl shook her head.

Emily opened up the paper at pages eight and nine, and Pearl gasped. There was a huge photograph of her in the middle of the double-page spread, smiling out at the reader. Across the top was the headline: YOUNG BLACK SWIMMER IS BEACON OF HOPE IN ELITIST SPORT.

'What the . . . ?' Pearl's voice trailed off.

'The whole article is about you,' Emily told her. 'And how you're the first black swimmer in British history to compete at the Olympics.'

Pearl stared. 'But I'm not. I mean . . .'

Emily nodded, frowning. 'No, you're not. There are other swimmers from black backgrounds representing Great Britain, but she seems to have ignored them.'

'Who?'

'The journalist.' Emily pointed to the by-line. 'Melissa Troughton. She also quotes you in the article.'

She held it out, and Pearl read:

An unassuming young lady, Pearl admits that she is 'very proud' of her achievement. 'I feel honoured to be a symbol for black people in British swimming,' she told me at a recent event.

Pearl's jaw dropped. 'I didn't say that!'

'But you did talk to her.'

'I – yes, at the Kellerman Club last week. But it was just a minute or two.'

'Why didn't you tell me?' asked Emily.

Pearl gulped. 'I forgot.' Which was partly true. She had slept so well that night, she'd woken feeling refreshed and eager on the Friday morning. The conversation with the journalist sat uncomfortably at the back of her mind, but she vaguely hoped that it wouldn't come to anything. And training had been such hard work that day that she had genuinely forgotten all about it by the weekend. 'Sorry.'

'Pearl, don't you remember that talk you had from the media consultant? You mustn't give an official interview without running it past me first. Especially one for a paper like this.'

Pearl hung her head. 'I never said that thing about being a symbol though.'

Emily sighed. 'You didn't have to. She made suggestions, and you agreed, right?'

Pearl tried to think. 'Well, she said something about being a symbol and I – I sort of mumbled.'

'But you didn't disagree.'

'Not exactly.'

'That's how she got away with it,' Emily told her. 'Some journalists can be very unscrupulous when it comes to getting a good story.' She held out the paper. 'You'd better read the whole thing.'

Pearl sat down, holding the paper in trembling hands.

At first glance, Pearl Okeke is like any other teenager. But beneath the surface lies a steely determination and an ambition to be the best. Pearl is the youngest, and the only black, member of the British Olympic Synchronized Swimming Team, which this year stands a reasonable chance of a medal, thanks to the unusual way the teams are selected. Only eight teams can compete in the Olympics, and each continent must be represented. Britain, placing ninth in last year's World Swimming Championships, was granted a place in the Olympics as the host nation. It will be the first time that Britain has entered the Olympic team synchro event.

With the weight of expectation, you might expect Miss Okeke (14) to be struggling, but her team manager is confident that Pearl is well up to the job. 'She was spotted at an early age,' confirms a source close to the team, 'and she's grown in strength and stamina remarkably quickly. She is unusually talented in this area and we predict great things for her future, possibly even graduating to solo swimming.'

Pearl's jaw dropped. Solo swimming? But she'd never wanted to perform on her own! 'Did you tell them I wanted to swim solo?'

'Of course not,' said Emily sharply. 'It says "a source", which could be anyone. She could even have asked one of the cleaners here. It's based on nothing.'

Pearl is Nigerian—

'I am not!' spluttered Pearl. 'I'm British!'

though she has lived all her life in the UK and devoted thousands of hours to UK swimming. She is shy about her cultural heritage, but her skill in the pool is evident, making her stand out from the crowd.

Pearl's heart sank even further. Standing out in a team was exactly the wrong thing to do – what on earth would the other girls think when they saw this?

An unassuming young lady, Pearl admits that she is 'very proud' of her achievement. 'I feel honoured to be a symbol for black people in British swimming,' she told me at a recent event.

With gang crime and poor literacy levels soaring

among black British youth, we need more youngsters like
Pearl to show that there is a better way.

This young woman is truly a black Pearl in the British
oyster.

Pearl put down the paper, feeling sick.

'It's not quite the kind of publicity we like for the
team,' Emily said gently, 'though obviously anything
that raises our profile . . .'

'But it makes me sound really arrogant – and all
that stuff about standing out . . .'

'Yes. She clearly has no idea what being in a
synchro team is about,' said Emily. 'Look, Pearl, it's
not your fault. I'm not blaming you at all. But take
this as an important lesson – don't talk to journalists
unless it's been set up officially. Many of them are very
respectful, but some will put words in your mouth, as
you've seen.' She reached over to take the paper from
Pearl. 'Go back to your training. We can't prevent the
other girls hearing about this, so I'll talk to everyone
at the end of your gym session. I'm sure they'll be
understanding.'

Pearl hoped so. She felt awful. What if the other
girls thought she wasn't fully committed to the team?
What if they believed that lie about her wanting to
perform solo? Or the one about her being some kind

of symbol for other black kids? *I don't want to be a symbol*, Pearl thought anxiously. *I just want to swim.*

♥

In the end, it wasn't as bad as Pearl had feared. The girls, initially cross about the inaccuracies and the fact that the article made it seem that Pearl was the best swimmer of them all, soon relaxed and resorted to taking the mickey out of her instead.

'Sorry, Pearl, did you want to go in front of me?' said Georgie as they headed for the changing rooms. 'Seeing as you're a beacon of hope?'

'Yeah, you can light the way for us,' added Primrose with a grin.

The other girls laughed. Pearl felt her face heat up, and she looked at the floor.

'Oh, come on.' Evie took her arm. 'We're only kidding. It is pretty funny.'

'But any time you want a solo spot, just let us know,' said Kat with a wink.

'I don't!' cried Pearl. 'I want to stay in the team!' She pulled away from Evie.

Jen shot a look at Kat. 'We know,' she said soothingly. 'It's all right, Pearl. The girls are just teasing.'

'Well, don't,' said Pearl, feeling tears prick behind

her eyes. 'I don't like it.' She felt like a child again, wishing she could go home.

'Stop it,' said Millie to the other girls, putting a protective arm around her friend's shoulders. 'She's really upset.'

'I wish I'd never gone to the Kellerman Club,' said Pearl mutinously. 'This has spoiled everything.'

Jen took charge. 'All right, everyone, I think you should all go and get changed, and Pearl and I will follow on in a minute. You too, Millie.'

Millie opened her mouth to object, but saw the look in Jen's eye and closed it again. Instead, she squeezed her friend's shoulder and went with the others.

'Tell Bonnie we'll be five minutes,' Jen called after them. Then she turned to Pearl. 'Come on. Let's find a quiet spot.'

There wasn't anywhere to sit, but the narrow corridor outside the squash courts was completely empty, and Jen stood facing Pearl. 'You can't swim if you're feeling all horrid inside. You know that.'

Pearl nodded, her eyes fixed on the rubber-surfaced floor.

'You've had articles written about you before, haven't you?'

'Yes, but only little ones. Not . . . This was a double-page spread, Jen! With a really gross picture of me!'

'I thought you looked quite nice,' said Jen with a smile.

'My shoulders look huge and my thighs are fat,' retorted Pearl.

'That's just the angle of the shot. You look fine. More importantly, it's a picture of you in your official British Synchro costume. It's a brilliant advert for the team.'

'By making me sound like I think I'm better than everyone else?' Pearl rubbed her right eye. It was wet.

'Nobody here thinks that though,' Jen told her. 'No one who knows you. You work for the team – we all do.'

'Huh.'

'Listen.' Jen folded her arms. 'Synchro is the sport everyone forgets about. In the swimming pecking order, we're way down the bottom. And we haven't got a great history. Look how far we've come in the past few years. If we win a medal . . . well . . .' She was silent for a moment. 'How amazing would that be? Wouldn't it just be the proudest moment of your life?'

Pearl nodded. 'Guess so.'

'What I'm trying to say – except I'm not saying it very well – is that basically, that article is kind of good for us.'

'What?' Pearl was startled.

'Two whole pages in a national newspaper about a synchronized swimmer!' Jen raised her eyebrows. 'I bet you most of the country didn't even know we had a synchro team. You and me, we live in this little bubble. We assume everyone outside the bubble knows how important synchro is and all that – but they don't. They still see us as pretty girls doing graceful ballet moves in the water. They have no idea how hard we work; how fit we have to be; how long we can hold our breath underwater while we do our routines. Other people perfect their strokes or their dives. We have to do it all, but synchro is still seen as a soft sport – probably most people wouldn't even call it a sport!

'I know the woman got half her facts wrong, but she did talk about the thousands of hours you've put into training. She mentioned how you had to have talent and skill to do what we do. The people who read that article, they'll be impressed. Yeah, they'll be taken in by all that "beacon of hope" rubbish, but they'll also have learned something about synchro. *And*' – Jen was struck by a new idea – 'maybe some young people will see the article and think that synchro sounds like a cool thing to do, and maybe they'll ask to go along to a synchro lesson and find out how much they like it. You never know, a future synchro champion might decide to take up the sport just because they read that article.'

Pearl was half smiling now. 'You're joking.'

'I'm not!' Jen smiled back at her. 'I'm saying that your story could be genuinely inspirational to someone else. You have to forget the stuff that journalist made up. We know it's not true. But some of it she got right, and it's important that people know more about us.' She looked up at the high ceiling. 'Apart from anything else, we cost money. Your article might find us a new sponsor.'

'Really?'

Jen shrugged. 'Who knows? But you can't let one little thing get you down. Synchro is more important than that. The *team* is more important.'

'I know.' Pearl felt guilty for overreacting. 'I just feel really stupid for talking to that journalist . . .'

Jen shook her head. 'Don't. It could have been any of us. You were caught off guard.'

'I didn't want to be rude . . .'

'Come on.' Jen held out her hand. 'Let's go get in the pool. The water will help.'

Pearl took her hand. 'Thanks, Jen.'

'No problem. But if you kick me in the back during the twist sequence, I'll tell everyone to start calling you a "beacon of hope" again.'

♥

Her mum was excited. 'You didn't tell me you were going to be in the paper!'

Pearl pulled a face. 'I didn't know.'

Linda gave her a hug. 'My little girl, an inspiration to other young people. I'm so proud of you!'

'Mum, it wasn't exactly accurate,' Pearl tried to explain, but her mum shook her head.

'I don't know what you're talking about, darling. It was all very complimentary. Fancy that person saying you were destined for a great future!'

Pearl sighed. 'Can we talk about something else?'

Linda noticed her expression. 'Of course, darling. I can tell you've had a long day.' She peered at her daughter. 'You look done in. Come on, let's get you home.'

Pearl was relieved that Edward wasn't in evidence as they walked through reception. Sometimes he was chatting to her mum when she came out, and although she could at least respond politely when he said hello, it always made her feel weird and slightly ashamed. It was over three weeks since the picnic and she still hadn't replied to Bailey's emails. There hadn't been one for six days now. She wondered what he had told his dad about the argument. Sometimes she thought she should reply and try to build a few bridges, but she was so tired by the evenings that she didn't have the energy to work out what to say.

When they got home, Linda insisted that Pearl lie on the sofa with a blanket. 'I'll get you some tea, darling.'

I'll just close my eyes, thought Pearl. *Just for a few minutes . . .*

♥

'Pearl. Pearl, sweetie. Your dinner's getting cold.'

'Hmm, what?' Pearl opened her eyes. 'I fell asleep?'

Her mum smiled. 'Looks like you needed it. You can go back to sleep after dinner, but you've got to eat.'

'Thanks, Mum.' Pearl sat up and tucked into the plate of pasta. 'Where's Harrison?'

'Round at Mark's, I think. Or maybe Tom's. He texted to say he would be out . . .' Linda hesitated. 'Darling, have you been in touch with Bailey at all?'

Pearl was startled. She'd been thinking about him only an hour ago! 'No, why?'

'Look, don't jump down my throat or anything – but I just wondered if you'd drop him a line.'

'Mum . . .'

Linda took a breath. 'Edward says he's still really upset about what he said to you. I don't know what it was, but he feels very guilty.'

'Good,' said Pearl shortly.

Linda put down her fork and looked earnestly at her daughter. 'Sweetheart, I know he made you angry, but it's not good to bear these grudges. I'm worried about you. Don't keep that resentment going – it'll eat away at you.'

'You don't know what he said,' Pearl told her, concentrating on her food.

'It's not just Bailey,' said Linda. 'What about your dad? We can't turn back the clock, but he's still your dad and he loves you.'

'How can you say that?' Pearl glared at her. 'How could he hurt me like that if he loved me?'

Her mum sighed. 'We all make mistakes. He's not my favourite person and he never will be again, but since meeting Edward ... well, I've found it a bit easier to let go of some of that anger. And I feel a lot better for it too. You should try it. Just give other people a bit of a chance; cut them a bit of slack. No one's perfect.'

'I'm not asking them to be perfect,' snapped Pearl. 'I just think some things are too bad to be forgiven.'

Linda bit her lip and looked down at her food. 'I'm sorry,' she said. 'It's probably my fault.'

'What do you mean?'

'You've had to do so much to support me since – since Winston left.'

Pearl blinked. It was the first time her mother had said her dad's name since he walked out.

'You've been so strong for me,' Linda went on, looking apologetic. 'I've leaned on you a lot. It's made you harden up. You've lost that soft side you used to have.' She pushed her pasta away. 'You were always driven, darling, but since he – Winston – left, you've become almost like a . . . like a robot. You're pushing yourself too hard; it's not good for you.'

'I'm practising for the Olympics,' said Pearl, frowning. 'I have to push myself hard.'

'But you've closed off all the soft side of yourself,' said her mum. 'You expect so much from yourself, it's like you want everyone else to live up to your standards. And they won't always, sweetie. Bailey may have said some stupid things. Your dad made a stupid mistake – and his timing was horrendous. But they both still care about you. They want to be friends. Can't you just give them another chance? For your own sake?'

Pearl finished the last forkful of pasta, though it

was hard to swallow. For some reason her throat had closed up. 'I don't want to talk about it, Mum. I'm really tired – I just want to go to bed.'

'Of course, love.' Linda gave her a little smile. 'I know you're under a lot of pressure right now.'

Pearl dragged herself up the stairs and fell onto her bed, pressing her face into the pillow. It felt like everyone wanted a piece of her at the moment – the team, her mum, Bailey, her dad . . . She wasn't sure there was enough to go round.

And deep inside, she knew her mum wouldn't have talked to her that way if she wasn't genuinely concerned. Bearing grudges – Linda was probably right. But the thought of ringing her dad or emailing Bailey . . . it was all too much.

Tomorrow, she decided, before sleep overcame her again. *Tomorrow I'll have a proper think about it . . .*

Chapter 12

you've already taken everything that mattered

'I've booked a coach to take us to the Park,' said Emily, waving a wad of paper. The girls were all gathered in the gym, perched on pieces of equipment and gazing at their manager, who was taking them through travel and accommodation plans for their move to the Olympic Park in only ten days. 'You'll get copies of all the paperwork to take home with you tonight, along with a list of suggested items to bring. Just because we're going to be in this country for the competition doesn't mean you can rely on nipping home to pick up something you forgot. Once we're in the Athletes' Village, we stay there. Understand?'

The girls nodded. Pearl felt a whirl of emotions. How could the move to the Athletes' Village have come round so quickly? Only yesterday it had felt like they still had months to go, and now . . .

'I can't believe it's really happening,' Hollie-Mae whispered to her. 'Can you?'

Pearl shook her head. 'We've been talking about the Olympics for so long, but somehow I never thought we'd actually get there. I mean – it feels unreal.'

'Back in that beautiful pool!' sighed Hollie-Mae, and Pearl felt a flutter of excitement. The team had been lucky enough to do some training at the Olympic Aquatics Centre, and of course they had participated in big sporting exhibitions there in the past year, but Pearl couldn't wait to see it again. It had a special feeling; a magical atmosphere. As though it knew it had been built especially for the Olympics, a place and time where dreams could be realized and broken.

The routines were rock solid now. They had two to perform: a technical and a 'free' routine. Pearl preferred the free routine because it was more imaginative, but at five minutes long it was extremely demanding, with long sequences underwater. They had gradually added and removed sections over the past ten months, until they had a routine that was as difficult as they could manage. Pearl knew that the Spanish and Russian teams were likely to have even harder routines, but there was nothing they could do about that.

The Athletes' Village was a massive residential development on the Park itself. The British Synchro team, as well as all the other Team GB swimmers, had been allocated apartments in the Village, where they would live and train alongside thousands of competitors from countries all around the world. And the competition itself was barely four weeks away!

The sense of excitement was palpable, even when the girls broke for lunch. 'I'm suddenly really nervous,' admitted Evie as she unwrapped her sandwiches at the table with Pearl and Millie. 'It's crazy.'

'I'm nervous too,' said Millie, 'and I won't even be competing!'

Pearl, despite her own fluttering excitement, felt sad for her best friend. 'Being reserve kind of sucks,' she said, squeezing Millie's hand.

Millie nodded. 'Yeah, it does. I've done all the training that you guys have done. I know every single move by every single one of you. I can slot in anywhere. But the only way I'll get to swim is if one of you is ill or injured, and that sucks too. I don't want any of you to get ill.'

Pearl felt a cold chill sweep up her back. *I really*

hope I don't get ill. That would be the most awful thing in the whole world – to miss the Olympics. She dug her spoon into her veggie rice. *I suppose at least if I got ill, Millie would have a chance to swim. But I'd be totally, completely gutted to miss out.*

'I wish more of my friends could come,' Evie said, changing the subject. 'But most of them didn't get tickets.'

'Mine too.' Millie cheered up. 'But hey, at least we'll be there – actually in the Athletes' Village, with all those amazing people!'

'Do you think Usain Bolt will be there?'

'Surely he's too famous to stay there,' said Pearl. 'Won't he be in a hotel?'

'Jen said at the last Olympics, Roger Federer was meant to be staying in the Village, but he got mobbed by so many people wanting his autograph that he moved out,' Millie told them.

'Tom Daley will be there though,' said Pearl slyly.

Millie blushed. 'Oh, shut up.'

All the girls knew that Millie had an enormous crush on the British diver, but whenever they'd met in the past, Millie had turned bright red and run in the opposite direction.

'I can't wait to wear our new costumes either,' Evie said. 'They look so amazing.'

The team had seen designs for the swimming costumes several months ago, but it had only been the week before that Emily had brought in a finished item. It had a halter neck and was studded with tiny diamantés in a Union Jack pattern. It glittered and sparkled under the lights of the pool. 'I'm terrified of damaging mine,' admitted Pearl. 'They're so expensive! Six hundred pounds for one swimming costume!'

'That's because they're so closely made to measure,' replied Millie. The costumes were made to fit each girl exactly, and all of them were made by one lady who had been making specialized swimming costumes for decades. 'But there is one spare if you do break yours.'

'Yes, but just one for the whole team!' exclaimed Pearl. 'Can you imagine if I made a hole in mine and then someone else broke theirs too? What would we do?'

Evie considered her seriously. 'You'd have to swim naked,' she said.

Millie, who was just taking a swig of water, gave a gigantic snort and coughed violently for the next ten minutes. By the time she'd calmed down, her face was bright red and her nose was streaming. Pearl and Evie were still giggling. 'Yeah, yeah,' she said crossly, 'laugh all you want. Just watch out for when I put arsenic in your soup the night before the competition.'

'Argh! Don't eat the soup!' Evie proclaimed, miming a dramatic death. 'She's going to kill us all!'

'Not *all* of you,' Millie pointed out. 'Just one . . .'

Pearl knew her friend was joking but she still felt bad that Millie wouldn't get to compete in the biggest event of their lives. It had been sixty-four years since the last Olympic Games were held in London. It really was the chance of a lifetime.

♥

Pearl got a lift home with Millie that evening, but when they pulled up outside her house, she frowned. There was an unfamiliar car parked in the driveway. It wasn't Edward's – she knew he drove a Saab. This was a BMW, all shiny, though the number plate show-ed it wasn't new.

'Who's that?' asked Millie curiously.

'Don't know.'

'Posh car,' commented Millie.

Pearl felt puzzled. 'Yeah. Maybe it's my uncle or something. He's into cars.'

'See you tomorrow!'

Pearl put her key in the front door and pushed. Instantly, she felt sick. There was a scent of aftershave in the air that she recognized only too well, and a familiar brown leather jacket hanging on the coat pegs. She looked around frantically. Where was her mum? But voices from upstairs soon gave her the answer – raised voices, arguing.

Pearl threw her bag on the floor and ran up the stairs two at a time. What was he *doing* here? Didn't he know he wasn't wanted?

Linda's bedroom door was wide open, and the two of them were standing on opposite sides of the bed, glaring at each other. 'You're lucky I didn't slice them into pieces,' Linda was saying.

Pearl stood in the doorway, feeling her knees weaken. She hadn't seen her dad for months, not since the day he'd walked out. He was wearing a new shirt, but the old jeans, the smell, his face, his hands – all were shockingly familiar.

He turned to her. 'Pearl!' For a moment she thought he was going to try to hug her, and she took an instinctive step backwards. His face fell slightly. 'You look so grown up!'

'What are you doing here?' she said, proud that her voice didn't wobble.

'Your dad came to get his things,' Linda said. Her eyes were shiny and her face was flushed. 'He should have been gone by now, but he was late getting here.'

Pearl's father gave a shrug. 'Traffic,' he said.

Pearl wondered if that was true or whether he'd deliberately arrived late so that he would have a chance of seeing her.

'I said he was lucky that I hadn't chopped all his clothes into tiny pieces,' Linda told her daughter. 'That I nearly had a massive bonfire in the garden and burned his CD collection.' She gave a strained laugh. *She's pretending she's OK with all this*, thought Pearl. *But she's not really – him being here is bringing it all back*.

Winston gave Pearl a smile; one that she didn't return. 'I've got a new flat now. It's got an attic, so I can take everything.'

I can take everything. 'You already have,' said Pearl, her eyes hard.

He looked puzzled. 'What do you mean?'

'You've already taken everything that mattered,' she went on. 'Walking out on us without a word – no sign, nothing. On the day I got into the team too.'

Winston cast a bewildered glance at Linda. 'What

is she talking about? We had loads of discussion before I left. Didn't you tell her?'

Linda bit her lip and said nothing.

'What?' Pearl was taken aback. 'Mum said you came home from work that evening and just said you were off!'

'Yes, but for weeks before, we'd been talking about how things weren't working out,' replied her father. 'Didn't she tell you?'

Pearl stared at her mother. 'No.'

'It doesn't matter,' said Linda. 'You left us.'

'Yeah,' said Pearl. 'Yeah, to be with that other woman. How is she – what was her name? Valerie?'

'Vivienne,' said Winston. He shifted his weight from one foot to the other. 'I don't know. We're not together any more.'

From the intake of breath her mother gave, Pearl guessed this was news to her too. 'So you left us for *nothing*? The whole family, split up for a woman you were only with for a couple of months? That's ... that's pathetic.'

'It's not as simple as that,' her father replied. 'Look, why don't we go downstairs and talk about this properly? I'm sure you've got questions ...'

Pearl shook her head. 'No. You know what? I don't. All I know is that you left us on the most important day of my life. I was picked for the Olympics, Dad – and I waited till I got home so that I could tell you to your face. I said to all the other girls, *I have to tell my dad first, face-to-face, because he's been the person who's supported me through all this. He's my biggest fan!* And so I didn't ring or anything. I waited till I got home – and *you weren't here.* You'd just . . . gone. Without a word!'

'I told your mum to tell you why,' Winston argued.

'I didn't *know* why!' retorted Linda. 'I *still* don't understand why! And now you say you've left this other woman too! Maybe I had a lucky escape!'

Pearl's father winced. 'That's not really fair—'

'Oh, you can't talk about being fair!' Pearl snapped. 'How do you think I felt? How do you think Harrison felt, or Mum? You didn't care about anyone except *yourself*, and that's totally not fair.'

'That's not true,' interrupted Winston. 'I talked it through with your mum many times—'

'You didn't talk it through with *me*, Dad!' Suddenly Pearl felt tears pricking at her eyes. Angrily she blinked them back. 'You can blame Mum all you like but you're the one who left! And that's why I never want to see you again – that's why I don't want to talk to you on the phone or anything. You can't make it right.'

Her father looked at her for a long moment. 'I'm sorry,' he said quietly. 'You're right, I should have talked to you. But I thought' – his eyes flicked to Linda – 'that your mother was talking to you. We both agreed that you needed to focus on your swimming and that you shouldn't be upset more than necessary.'

Pearl snorted.

'I know, I know. But I didn't realize that *that* was going to be the day you found out whether you'd been selected for the team. And I couldn't stay any longer – your mum and I had agreed that.'

Pearl glanced at her mother, shocked. *Agreed?* Linda had *known* that he was going to leave that day?

Her father sighed. 'If I could turn back time, I'd do a lot of things differently, Pearl. I can only say I'm sorry again.'

'Huh.' But Pearl was feeling bewildered. Was there more to her dad's leaving than she had thought? Had her mum been keeping something from her?

Winston picked up a couple of bags, full to bursting with his clothes. 'I'd better go,' he said. 'I didn't mean to . . . Well, I'd better go. But I just want to say I've been following all your news on the British Synchro website, and all the media coverage too. I'm so proud of you for making the team, and I'm going to do everything I can to see you swim.'

Pearl didn't know what to say. She didn't want him to come and watch, did she? But he had always come when she'd competed at junior levels – he'd always been the one in the crowd, cheering for her. Wouldn't it be weird to compete at the Games without him there? Oh, now she didn't know *what* to think or how to feel!

Chapter 13

don't shut people out

'Cup of tea?' Linda said brightly, as soon as Winston had gone.

Pearl stared at her. 'Mum, what was he talking about? You told me it was a complete shock when he left. You said you had no warning.'

Her mother looked everywhere but at Pearl. 'Come on,' she urged, 'let's get a cup of tea.' She turned and went downstairs.

Pearl had no choice but to follow her, but her head was a whirl. She and her mum had become so close over the past few months . . . had it all been based on a lie? When Mum said she couldn't understand why Dad had left – had she been lying?

'Mum . . .'

Linda clicked on the kettle and got out two mugs. 'I thought he'd be gone by the time you got home,' she said apologetically. 'So typical of him to mess things up again.'

'*Mum*.'

'What?'

'You *know* what!' Pearl almost cried in frustration. 'What aren't you telling me? Was Dad right? Did you talk about him leaving before he went? Did you know, all along, that he was walking out on us?'

'Oh, what difference does it make?' Linda shot a guilty look at her daughter. 'He left, didn't he? Does it really matter whether I knew in advance or not?'

'Of *course* it matters! You said it was out of the blue – and now it turns out you knew all along! Why didn't you tell me?'

'Because I hoped he wouldn't really do it, all right?' Linda snapped. She glared at Pearl. '*Yes*, we talked about it. He wasn't happy. I knew that. We both knew it hadn't been working for ages. He talked about this other woman – Vivienne – and I knew he was having an affair. He kept saying he would end it, but after a while he changed his mind and started saying he didn't think our marriage was worth saving . . . I just thought he needed space. I thought, if I backed off for a bit, he'd see what he really had with us – his family. I tried to be sympathetic, to agree to whatever he wanted. I reckoned that would make him see how much I wanted this all to work out OK – but instead he thought I didn't care.'

'But why didn't you tell me any of this?' asked Pearl, bewildered.

The kettle clicked off and Linda turned away. 'How could I?' she said, and her voice sounded wobbly. 'You were so busy with your training. And you and I weren't that close – not back then. You were always your dad's daughter. He and you – well, you had a bond, didn't you? I didn't want to upset that. And, like I say, I kept hoping it would work out all right in the end.'

Pearl bit her lip. She could see why her mum had kept things from her, but she wished now that she hadn't. 'Then why didn't you tell me when he left? When I came home and he'd gone, and you said he'd just left us without a word?'

Linda poured out the hot water and stirred the tea bags before she answered. 'Maybe I got it wrong,' she said, and gave a big sigh. 'I was angry, Pearl. And so sad – sad for all of us, but especially for myself. And it *was* a shock. He'd said he was leaving, but until he actually walked out of the door, I didn't believe him. I honestly, honestly, thought he'd come back.' She turned, and Pearl saw the tears on her cheeks. 'I'm so sorry, my darling,' she said softly. 'I never meant to lie to you. But I was so hurt and so angry, and maybe it made me feel better to tell you I hadn't seen it coming. I wanted you to be angry with him too.' She wiped her face. 'Maybe,' she added quietly, 'I thought that if I told you the truth, you'd be angry with *me* instead – for not trying harder to make him stay. And I couldn't bear that.'

There was a pause. Pearl felt a great weight sink through her, as though the answers were falling from her shoulders right through her feet to the floor. 'Oh,' she said, unable to think of anything else to say. How could she be angry with her mum over this? Linda shouldn't have lied to her – she should have trusted Pearl with the truth – but Pearl had to acknowledge that if she'd known . . . would she have turned against her mum? Would she have been willing to support her and become such a close friend, knowing that her mum could have protected her from the shock of her dad's leaving? 'What about Harrison?' she asked suddenly. 'Did he know?'

Linda reached for the milk in the fridge door. 'I don't know. I think he suspected . . . He heard us talking once, but he never mentioned it to me. But maybe that's why he's still angry with me. Maybe he thinks I should have done more.'

'I'm not sure he's angry with you,' Pearl considered. 'I think maybe he's angry with everyone.'

'You could be right.' Linda poured out the tea and sighed again. 'Maybe I should try to get him to sit down and talk to me. We could clear the air.' She looked hopefully at Pearl. 'But we're all right, aren't we? You and me? I mean . . .'

Pearl looked down at the floor. 'Yeah, Mum. We're all right. I just – I just feel really sad about it all.'

'Me too, honey.' Linda gave her a hug. 'Me too.'

♥

It had been so long since Bailey had emailed Pearl that when she checked her inbox the next evening and saw his name, she felt a jolt of anticipation. She hadn't expected to hear from him again – but maybe it was time to make up?

Hi Pearl
I hope you like the attached. It's an article I've just written for the next Parchester *Youth Voice* magazine

(I've got a permanent job as a Junior Reporter there now). I wanted to show it to you because it was sort of inspired by our conversation at the park.

Best wishes,

Bailey

Inspired by their conversation at the park? Pearl wasn't sure she liked the sound of that at all. She flexed her fingers before clicking on the attachment.

WHAT ABOUT THE KIDS?
By Bailey Ross, Junior Reporter

Divorce is so common these days, people are almost blasé about it. Everyone knows the statistics; no one is shocked. Until it happens to you.

No, I'm not divorced. I'm not even old enough to be married. But my parents got divorced a couple of years back, and even though I knew it was coming, it was still a shock.

I met someone recently whose parents are going through a divorce. It reminded me just how scary everything is to start with. Your world is suddenly turned upside-down; the word 'family' doesn't mean the same thing any more – or does it have a meaning at all? You start to question everything, and it changes the way you look at your life and the people in it.

Divorce does that to kids, you see. We might understand that our parents are better off apart, but that doesn't mean that *we're* better off without one of them. And don't fob me off with the whole, 'You see your dad/mum every other weekend' stuff. It's not the same. Basically, you start off with two parents who love each other and who love you – and then one of them fades out of everyday life. They're not there in the morning, when you get up. They're not there when you get home from school. They're not there to defuse arguments with the remaining parent; to take you down to the park/shop/cinema when the other parent is busy. They're just not a part of your life in the way they were before.

And that really hurts. It doesn't matter how amicable the split was: my parents 'drifted apart', as they like to put it; there were no massive rows. But I still miss my mum. I know it wasn't my fault she left; I know it wasn't anybody's fault, but I still sometimes wonder if there was something I could have done; something I could have said, that would have kept them together.

Having parents who live apart can have its advantages, of course. I get twice the number of presents at Christmas and birthdays. I get 'special treats' more often, because my mum particularly feels she needs to make the most of the 'quality time' we spend together. My parents are happier apart, and I've had to accept that. And maybe over time, I'll come to believe that I'm happier with them apart too, but it hasn't happened yet.

If I could say one thing to that girl, I'd say this: stuff happens. And nobody's perfect. People say and do things they don't really mean, and sometimes all they want is for you to give them a second chance. That can apply to friends, siblings and parents. Don't shut people out because something bad has happened: that's when you need friends and family the most.

Pearl sat back, feeling quite emotional. How did Bailey know so exactly what to say? How did he get to be so clever with words? It was almost as if he'd been there, watching while she and her mum had talked! She hit 'reply' and began to type, hardly thinking about what she was saying.

Bailey, thank you so much for this article. I really get it. I thought you were totally sorted about your parents. I think you're really brave to write about it like this, for everyone to see. Something really bizarre happened yesterday. Dad came back to get his stuff and it turns out that – well, Mum hasn't been telling me everything. Like the fact that they were having problems before he left – I didn't know any of that. He's not with the other woman any more, but he's not coming back either. I thought I didn't want him back but that was because I was so mad at him. Now . . . I don't know. It seems I was mad at him for the wrong reasons, but he still left, didn't he?

Anyway, thanks again. The article really helped. And I'm sorry. I was so worried about protecting Mum, I think maybe I overreacted to what you said. I know you wouldn't have said it if you'd known.

I'd like to be friends again. If you want.

Pearl

She hit 'send' and sat back, a wave of relief washing through her. It felt good, to be apologizing to Bailey. It was right to forgive him. He wasn't a bad person. She still wasn't sure how she felt about his father. Even more now, she was convinced that Mum shouldn't be seeing someone new. But maybe Edward was nicer than she'd given him credit for?

Having sent the email, another thought occurred to her. Harrison had come in late the evening before, so he had missed the whole encounter with their dad and Pearl's subsequent chat with Linda. But he was in his bedroom now, so it might be a good time to try to talk to him too. While she was feeling optimistic about building bridges, she might as well try to build one with her brother!

She knocked on Harrison's door.

'What?' came the grumpy reply.

Pearl pushed open the door a little. 'It's me. Can I come in?'

'Suppose so.' Her brother was sitting on his bed, surrounded by textbooks. In his arms was his beloved electric guitar, unplugged. Pearl suspected that the books were only for show; he'd actually been playing the guitar instead of revising again.

She came in, closed the door and leaned against it. 'I wanted to say sorry.'

For once, Harrison looked surprised. 'What for?'

'For not talking to you much. I mean – I know you don't really like talking to me or Mum, but I think I should have made more of an effort.'

Harrison shuffled slightly on his bed. 'Oh.'

'You know Dad came back yesterday?'

Harrison nodded. 'Mum said.'

'Well, it sounds like Mum didn't tell me – us – the truth. That she and Dad had been having problems before he left.' She looked at him curiously. 'Did *you* know?'

Her brother shrugged. 'Sort of. It was kind of obvious, really.'

'Was it?' Pearl was taken aback. 'I didn't notice anything.'

'Yeah, well, you were busy with your training and that. You weren't really here.'

'I was.' She felt defensive. 'Why didn't you say something?'

'Not my business. But I could see things were getting worse. Nothing I could do about it, especially as Mum was being so stupid about the whole thing.'

'What do you mean?'

He rested his hand on the strings of his guitar. 'Trying to pretend nothing was happening. Being all sweetness and light to Dad when it annoyed him so much.'

Pearl swallowed. 'She told me she thought that if she was extra nice to him, he wouldn't leave.'

'Yeah, well, just sticking her head in the sand, wasn't she? As usual.'

'Are you mad at her?'

He paused. 'A bit. I was to start with. I dunno. It annoys me when she plays the victim.'

'Victim?'

'Yeah, like she was the wronged party the whole time. When if she'd made a bit more of an effort . . . I dunno.'

'Do you think . . .' Pearl struggled to finish. 'Do you think Dad might have stayed?'

He met her gaze squarely for the first time. 'Probably not. But we'll never know, will we?'

♥

She felt unmistakably lighter. Talking to Harrison had been a good thing. Before she got into bed, she checked the netbook again, just in case there was a message from Bailey. There wasn't, and her heart sank, but just as she was hovering over the 'shut down' button, it pinged in.

Friends is cool ☺ Can we meet? B

Pearl stared at it. Meet? But there was no time! In only a matter of days she would be moving into the

Athletes' Village and then she'd be on a tight training programme, with little time off. How frustrating! Suddenly she really, really wanted to see him. But it was too late.

If only she'd forgiven him weeks ago!

Chapter 14

I will remember this

'Wow!' Pearl stood on the balcony and gazed out over the Olympic Park. 'This is amazing.'

She was sharing an apartment with Millie and Evie, and their arrival in the Athletes' Village had been punctuated with squeals of delight. Pearl had the vague idea they were supposed to be all grown up and professional about it, but everything was just too exciting. Over to their right was the strange crisp-shaped roof of the Velodrome, its copper tiling glowing in the sun. Over to the left, towering above most of the other buildings, was the mighty Olympic Stadium. And almost directly in front of them, only ten minutes' walk away, was the Aquatics Centre. Pearl swallowed, gazing at its wave-like roof and vertical 'wings' at the side.

'How many did they say it could hold?' asked Evie in a small voice.

'Seventeen and a half thousand,' replied Millie.

'It looks even bigger from here,' said Evie, and Pearl nodded.

What would it be like to swim in front of seventeen and a half thousand people, all of them yelling for their own team? They'd been here before, but never when the Centre was completely full. Pearl couldn't imagine how loud it would be. Would people be allowed to take flash photographs? Would she be able to shut it all out successfully and concentrate on the swimming? The Games were the pinnacle of all sporting events. If you told someone you had a World Championship swimming medal, they'd be impressed, but not as impressed as they'd be by an Olympic medal. And this was in front of a British crowd too!

'Is anyone else really, really terrified?' asked Evie in a whisper.

'Yup,' said Pearl.

'I'm terrified and I'm not even swimming,' added Millie, gazing at the beautiful building.

'Everything's here,' said Evie. 'Everything.'

'Well, not quite everything,' Pearl disagreed. 'There's no sailing or football or gymnastics . . .'

'That's true,' said Millie. 'There are loads of other

venues, aren't there? How many did they say at our orientation talk?'

'Can't remember.'

'Hellooo!' Kat and Lizzie stuck their heads round the door. 'You ready? We've got to get all the way over to the practice pools.'

The girls grabbed their towels and costumes. Pearl felt her heart leap in excitement. She'd been away from home many times in the past: synchro camps were almost always abroad, and of course there were the exhibitions and competitions – but she'd never taken part in anything as monumental as this. As they made their way down the stairs, snatches of conversation floated out from other rooms and apartments, in a mixture of languages. Pearl recognized French, Russian and Spanish, but the others were just a jumble of sounds. A tall, good-looking boy with wide, strong shoulders came out into the stairwell, laughing at something his friend said. He bumped into Millie, who stumbled and grabbed the banister for support. The boy exclaimed in some foreign language and then said, 'I so sorry. Sorry!'

'That's all right,' said Millie.

He smiled at her and her face reddened as she followed the others down the stairs. Pearl grinned at her when they reached the bottom. 'He was pretty cute.'

'Shut up,' Millie told her cheerfully.

The sun was out as they made their way across the Park, heading through the green area. 'I can't believe how much those trees have grown,' commented Kat.

'I remember when they were put in,' said Lizzie.

'You sound as though you were actually here,' said Evie with a laugh.

'I can't help it,' replied Lizzie. 'I feel, in some strange kind of way, as though this place is – well, it's almost my back garden. Do you know what I mean? It's *ours*, it's British. We were here a year ago, back before everything was finished and shiny. Way before any of the overseas teams. It makes me feel kind of . . .'

'Smug?' suggested Kat, with a smirk.

'No, no – proud.' Lizzie gave her twin a look. 'Stop taking the mickey out of me. I'm being serious here.'

'I know exactly what you mean,' said Pearl. 'I feel the same way. Like it belongs to us in a way; to all British athletes.'

'Listen to you two!' exclaimed Kat. 'Next thing you know you'll be singing the national anthem!'

Millie immediately broke into song, dissolving halfway through the first verse when she realized she didn't know all the words. 'You'll have to learn them all before the competition starts,' Evie told her, 'just in case we win a medal!'

Millie laughed. 'You planning on winning gold, Evie? You only get your anthem played if you win gold.'

'Hey, I never said I wasn't ambitious.' Evie grinned.

Millie's face dropped. 'Yeah, that's all very well, but some of us won't get a chance to swim at all.'

There was an awkward silence. 'Isn't that Sue Barker?' asked Kat suddenly. 'Over there, in the yellow suit.'

'It is,' said Evie, with a nod. 'My dad fancies her.'

'Wonder what she's doing here,' said Lizzie. 'She's commentating on the tennis, but that's all at Wimbledon.'

'Are you guys going to try to see anything else while you're here?' asked Evie.

'Will we get in to anything if we haven't booked tickets?' wondered Pearl.

'Worth asking.'

They were within sight of the huge temporary

structure that housed the two practice pools on the edge of the Park. 'Not as pretty as the Aquatics Centre,' said Lizzie with a sigh. 'Never mind, we'll get our chance.'

Bonnie was waiting for them, along with Emily and the rest of the girls. 'We're not late, are we?' asked Pearl anxiously.

Bonnie shook her head. 'No, you're exactly on time. It's good, keep it up. We only get certain time slots, and we can't over-run by even a minute. Everyone has to have a turn in the pool, and as you can see, we're not the only ones here.'

They headed for the locker rooms and Pearl could see what Bonnie meant. There were girls everywhere, many of whom looked familiar from overseas training camps and other competitions. Outside in the corridors, they came across a few boys and men with powerful shoulders and arms from speed swimming.

'Do you get the feeling people are staring at you?' Millie murmured to Pearl as they changed.

Pearl glanced around surreptitiously. 'Sort of, but I think they're staring at everyone. I mean, we're staring too. Sizing up the competition.'

'That's true. Have you seen the Russians yet? Or the Spanish?'

'No, but they'll be here at some point. We're bound to run into them.'

'I hope we don't see Carolina,' muttered Evie. 'That would be kind of awkward.'

The training session went well, though Pearl felt twice as exhausted by the end of it. Training in front of other teams put that much more pressure on – it felt as though they had to do their absolute best in every single move because other people were watching. *Which is silly*, Pearl told herself, *because it's not as though we're going to change things now. We know the routines inside out and we know we can do them well. So why bother about what other people think?* But still she couldn't help looking around as they got out of the pool to see if any of their rivals had been observing.

The Spanish synchro team arrived just as they were leaving the locker room. There were polite hellos and nods of recognition between the girls. 'They look so stuck up,' whispered Millie to Pearl as they went out to the reception area. 'Like they know they're the best and can look down on everyone else.'

'They probably get it from Carolina,' said Evie in a low voice. She shuddered. 'Good thing we haven't seen her.'

'I think you're imagining things,' Pearl told them. 'One of them gave me a really nice smile.'

Millie shook her head. 'I'm going mad, I think. It's all this competition – it makes me see things that aren't there.'

Evie put her arm around Millie's shoulders. 'It's all right, Mills. Chill out. We've got days to go before the competition starts. You mustn't get yourself in a fuss.'

Millie sighed and smiled. 'Sorry. You're right, of course. I'll shut up now. What's on the schedule for the rest of the day?'

♥

Only two days later, Pearl found herself standing with thousands of other athletes as they waited to enter the Olympic Stadium as part of the enormous Opening Ceremony. Georgie, just in front of her, was jiggling from one foot to the other.

'What's the matter?' Pearl hissed.

'I need a wee!' Georgie whispered back.

'Why didn't you go before we left the Village?'

'I did!' said Georgie, agonized. 'I need to go again!'

Pearl looked around helplessly. As far as she

could see, athletes were waiting patiently, dressed in their national team kit. In only a few minutes, they would start to walk into the stadium as part of a great parade, each team following a flag-bearer waving their national flag. As the host nation, Team GB would be last into the stadium. 'You've got time to go now,' Pearl told Georgie. 'Go on. It'll take ages for everyone to get in – you know how many countries we've got to get through before it's our turn.'

'What if I miss it?' asked Georgie, her red hair glinting in the floodlights.

'Better than wetting yourself in front of millions,' advised Kat, who had overheard. 'Go on, Georgie, while there's still time.'

'All right.' Georgie headed off, pushing her way through. 'Don't go without me!'

'We'll have to keep an eye out for her,' Kat said to Pearl. 'We might have moved by the time she gets back.'

Pearl turned to speak to Millie, but her friend had a strange frozen expression on her face. 'Mills? What is it?'

'Erk,' said Millie.

'Are you OK?'

'Mmm-hhm-mmm.'

Pearl turned to see what she was looking at. Less than two metres away was Tom Daley, the British diver. He was looking particularly tanned and gorgeous this evening. 'Oh,' said Pearl, instantly understanding.

Millie grabbed her hand so tightly it hurt. 'Don't look – *don't look*!'

'Ow!'

'He'll see us!'

Pearl laughed. 'Millie, he knows who we are anyway. We see him around all the time at competitions.'

'Yes, but he's not usually just *standing* there looking . . . looking *cute*!'

'All right,' said Pearl, taking pity on her. She extracted her hand from Millie's grasp and rubbed it. 'I won't look. But there's no reason why you shouldn't just have a conversation with him sometime, Mills. He is just a person, you know.'

Millie shook her head decisively. 'No, he isn't.'

Pearl gave up. She looked over towards the entrance, but all she could see were rows and rows of heads. 'I wish we could see the ceremony,' she said with a sigh. 'Such a shame we have to miss the dancing and the costumes and all that stuff.'

'There'll be a bit more when we're standing inside,'

Evie told her. 'There usually is. Look, they've started going in.'

The long queue moved very slowly forward. People with radio headsets, dressed in black, moved among them, stopping and starting the groups. Georgie reappeared, looking relieved and surprised. 'You're still in the same place!' she said, out of breath. 'I wouldn't have run all the way there and back if I'd known!'

But it was finally their turn, and Pearl felt her heart beat faster as they approached the massive archway. The noise of the crowds grew louder and louder until she felt it fill her head completely. The lights grew brighter, and then she was inside the stadium and it was like being inside the jaws of a roaring lion. Pearl put one foot in front of the other but she was barely aware of walking; all she could see and feel was the immense space and the enormous number of people, some very far away, but all of them cheering and shouting. *I will remember this*, she said to herself. *Years from now, I'll be able to look back on this. I can tell my children and my grandchildren about how I walked out in front of thousands of people, and millions more watching on television all around the world, to represent my country*. Her eyes filled with tears. *I'm so lucky*, she thought. *Lucky to be here, doing what I love in front of people cheering me on.* She stumbled slightly, and the jolt made her blink. *But first I must make sure I don't break my ankle on international television. That would* not *be something to be proud of!*

♥

Training was hard, though their time in the pool was necessarily limited. The intensive training the team had done back at their base stood them in good stead, and Pearl found herself becoming more and more confident as the days went by. The only thing that marred the excitement was the constant dread of injury. Several of the girls had long-standing problems, and it didn't take much to trigger a return of the familiar pain. The team physio had travelled with them, but there was only so much strapping-up a body could take. Pearl knew she had been lucky not to sustain anything too serious so far, but she could tell from the occasional grimaces from the other girls that sheer willpower was keeping them at performance level.

It didn't help that there was so much going on to distract them. 'It's good for you,' Bonnie told them firmly. 'If you can keep your focus during these few days, it will be excellent training for the competition. You'll need to be able to shut everything out and concentrate only on the routine.' The girls nodded seriously and slipped into the water for another practice session.

In a run-through of the free routine one afternoon, Pearl caught a glimpse of someone who looked like her father, sitting in the gallery. It was only a split second, but that moment of distraction cost Pearl her focus, and Primrose's leg, kicking sharply, hit her right across the face.

Pearl felt a sudden blinding pain across her nose and cheek, and immediately struck out for the side. Some injuries you swam through; but if there was any chance her nose was going to bleed, she needed to get out of the water quick. Blood in the pool would mean training was suspended while the water was cleaned, and time was too precious for that. It was hard to swim when her eyes were streaming and she could barely tell which was the closest side, but as soon as her fingers touched the solid surface, she hauled herself out, hand clamped to her nose.

The music stopped abruptly and Bonnie came running over. 'Pearl, you all right? Is it your nose?'

Pearl nodded, still squinting through the pain radiating across her cheekbone.

'Is it bleeding? Let me see.'

Out of nowhere, two first aiders appeared with a green kit bag. But Pearl's nose, mercifully, was not bleeding, and after a few moments to establish that, Pearl was given an ice-pack to hold to her cheek.

Bonnie seemed relieved. 'You could have broken your nose, Pearl. What happened?'

Pearl shrugged, too embarrassed to admit that she'd been distracted by someone who looked like her dad. 'Just lost focus. Sorry, I don't know why.'

Bonnie looked at her for a moment. 'Hmm. It's not like you. Maybe we should have a chat later.'

'I'm fine, Bonnie.' Pearl was alarmed. She didn't want Bonnie to think she was losing her nerve! 'Honestly. I just looked away for a second and my timing went. It won't happen again.'

'Your cheek may well swell up,' one of the first aiders told her. 'A bump like that across the cheekbone . . .'

'What about her eye?' asked Bonnie. 'If her cheek swells up, will she be able to see all right?'

The first aider shook her head. 'Too early to say.'

Pearl felt the world tip sideways. If her eye swelled

and she couldn't see properly... that would mean she'd be out of the team for definite. They wouldn't let her swim if she didn't have perfect vision. Her head throbbed.

'Right.' Bonnie made a decision. 'Training's over for you today, Pearl. I want you to get changed and then report straight to the medical officer for a full examination. I'll send someone along to keep you company. Then you're to go straight back to your apartment and rest, all right?'

Pearl, panic sweeping through her, nodded. Blurrily, behind Bonnie she could see the anxious faces of the rest of the team peering over the edge of the pool. Primrose was biting her nails and looking frightened. Pearl wanted to say it wasn't her fault, but she was horribly afraid she might cry, so she just got up and headed for the changing area, one of the first aiders by her side urging her to walk slowly.

Within a couple of hours, Pearl's face was indeed swelling. The bash to her cheekbone had resulted in a dark patch which the medical officer said was a bruise; it would turn even darker before it healed completely. Pearl sat miserably on the sofa in her apartment and flicked through the TV channels, picking up a mirror every five minutes to examine her face.

Millie and Evie had come back as soon as they

could, keen to make sure their friend was OK. But Pearl found it difficult to talk to Millie, even though she was her best friend. Millie was also the team reserve, and if Pearl couldn't swim in the competition, Millie would be taking her place. Pearl knew her friend would be devastated on her behalf if she wasn't allowed to swim; but she also knew how badly Millie wanted to swim herself.

Millie seemed to sense Pearl's unease. 'I don't want to replace you,' she said sincerely. 'Anyone but you.'

'Hey!' said Evie.

'You know what I mean,' went on Millie. 'You're my best friend. You deserve to swim. I would be gutted for you.'

Pearl nodded, feeling tears sting her eyes. She grabbed the mirror to see if the swelling had got any worse.

'We've got to go down and get some lunch,' said Evie after an uncomfortable moment. 'You coming?'

'I'm not hungry.'

'We'll bring you some sandwiches,' Millie told her, sounding sympathetic.

Pearl shrugged. 'OK.' She knew she was being ungrateful, but she couldn't help it. Her whole future career could be at stake because she lost concentration for a split second. If she couldn't swim at the Olympics . . . well, she'd never have another chance like this one. To swim in London, in front of a home crowd, in the biggest sporting competition in the world – how would she ever get over it if she couldn't take part?

She managed to hold it together until the other two left, and then she threw herself onto the sofa cushions, sobbing and sobbing until it felt like she'd cried her own swimming pool.

When it was all over, Pearl sat up, dried her eyes and blew her nose. Her face was even puffier than it had been before, but she did at least feel a little better. Now she just felt lonely. Who could she talk to? Curiously, the first person she thought of was Bailey – but that was silly, wasn't it? They hadn't managed to meet before Pearl had moved to the Athletes' Village, and although they'd exchanged some friendly emails, it wasn't as though she really knew him very well.

She reached for her phone and, without even thinking, dialled home.

'Hello?'

'Hi, Mum, it's me.'

'Pearl, darling! I was going to call you this evening. How's it going?'

Pearl screwed up her nose, making her cheek ache.

'Not so good. I . . . I had a bit of an accident.'

'What! What kind of accident?' Linda's voice was immediately panicked.

'No, no, Mum, nothing like that – it's not that bad!' Pearl hastily reassured her. 'I just – I lost concentration in the pool and got kicked in the face.'

'Oh, darling, are you all right?'

'Yeah. I didn't break my nose or anything. But my face is swelling up, and they say if it gets too swollen round my eye . . .' Pearl gulped.

Her mother understood immediately. 'Oh, Pearl, love. Oh, darling. When will you know how bad it's going to be?'

Pearl felt a wave of relief; her mother knew how she was feeling. Since the day her dad had turned up, Pearl had felt a bit distanced from her mum; unwilling to forgive her for not telling the whole truth. But speaking to her on the phone now, that was all forgotten, and she just knew that her mum was the best person to call. 'This evening, probably. I've got to go back to the medical team and get an assessment.'

'How does it look at the moment? How long ago did it happen?'

Pearl explained everything, from the moment she'd felt Primrose's leg connect with her cheek, to the difficulties with Millie in the apartment. 'And I feel really bad,' she concluded, 'because Millie's my best friend and if I can't swim it's the biggest ever opportunity for her, so either way it would be a *good* thing, wouldn't it . . . ?'

Linda was silent for a moment. Then she said, 'Pearl, that's a very noble thing to say but I know you don't really feel like that. You're a competitor; you want to take part. It's all right, darling, you don't have to pretend to me. I know how much it all means to you, and it must be twice as hard because Millie's such a good friend.'

Pearl felt her lip wobble. 'Thanks, Mum.'

'Think positive, darling. I'm sure you'll still be able to compete. Lots of ice and rest – have you got any arnica? Take that too. And try not to worry. I expect by tomorrow morning you'll be fine.'

'Yeah. Yes, you're right. Thanks, Mum, you always know the right thing to say.'

A sigh came down the phone. 'Oh, not always, love. I just make it up as I go along, like everyone else. But I know *you*, and I care about you and Harrison more than anything else in the world. Everything I do and say, I have your best interests at heart. I hope you believe that.'

'I do, Mum.'

When Millie and Evie came back with the

sandwiches and a bottle of Coke, Pearl smiled at them. 'Thanks, guys. I'm feeling a bit better now. Sorry I was grumpy.'

'No need to apologize,' Evie told her. 'We know how you feel.'

'I know. And I'm going to come and watch training this afternoon. I don't want to sit on my own and feel miserable all the time. You're my friends.'

'Group hug!' cried Millie.

As they threw their arms around each other, Pearl thought how lucky she was to have such great friends. And how, even if the worst happened, there would be a small silver lining for Millie.

But she hoped desperately that she would still be allowed to swim.

Chapter 15

two more sleeps

'It's looking all right,' said the doctor, studying Pearl's face intently. She smiled. 'There's a nasty mark but you can cover it with all that thick make-up you girls have to wear. The swelling isn't bad and it won't get any worse now – in fact, in a couple more days it'll probably have gone down completely. When's your first competition?'

'Three days' time,' Pearl said, her heart thumping with relief.

The doctor nodded. 'Well, you've got the go-ahead from me.'

Pearl punched the air as she left the medical office. Thank goodness for that! She felt a momentary qualm as she thought how disappointed Millie would be, but the faint twinge couldn't sweep away the huge feeling of relief and excitement. *Now*, she told herself, *you just have to make sure you don't do anything else stupid in the next few days . . .*

♥

The rest of the team was pleased to have her back, and Pearl could tell that Bonnie and Emily were relieved too. Millie was an excellent swimmer, but if she had had to slot in at this late hour, it would have been hard work for everyone.

Millie had congratulated Pearl like everyone else, but the next morning Pearl spotted that her eyes were red and felt sorry for her. What a horrible blow for her friend. She just wished there was something she could do.

There was a lot of training, but there were spare hours too, and Pearl was genuinely pleased to see her mum two days before the competition. Linda had brought Harrison along, since his exams had finished, and the three of them went out for dinner at a little restaurant in Greenwich. Harrison, usually silent, was on good form, and Pearl found herself laughing at his awful jokes in a way she hadn't for months. They even managed to talk about a good family holiday from three years ago without any awkward moments.

Pearl hesitated before asking since she didn't want to spoil the atmosphere. 'Are you still seeing Edward?'

Linda shot a quick glance at Harrison, who was digging into a large bowl of sticky toffee pudding. 'Yes,' she said, 'but . . . I don't know. Things aren't quite as good as they were.'

'Oh, really?' Pearl tried to sound casual.

'Yeah. I don't know what it is, exactly,' her mum went on. 'He's a lovely man, but I'm not sure he's the one for me.'

Pearl decided not to say any more about it, and the conversation moved on. But secretly she was relieved to hear that her mum was taking things more slowly. It didn't sound like she was going to rush into another marriage any time soon, at least!

'Harrison's got a girlfriend,' Linda said suddenly.

Pearl, astonished, turned to her brother, whose skin had darkened in a blush. 'Really? Who?'

'*Mum* . . .' Harrison looked acutely embarrassed.

'What? She's lovely. And she's got an amazing voice, Pearl – you should hear her. I caught the end of one of their rehearsals. She sounds just like Alexandra Burke.'

Pearl raised her eyebrows.

'New singer for the band,' said Harrison gruffly. 'She's called Malaika.'

'That's a nice name,' said Pearl. 'Is she at your school?'

'No.'

'OK.' Pearl sensed she wasn't going to get anything else out of him, but she was amused. Harrison with a girlfriend! And one their mother approved of too! Astonishing!

As they finished their meal, Linda reached under the table and produced a shiny wrapped box. 'We brought you a good luck present,' she told Pearl.

'You didn't have to do that . . .'

'I wanted to get you a cuddly bear,' her mother went on, 'but Harrison told me that would be a stupid present.'

Harrison made a face. 'She's *fourteen*, not four.'

Pearl laughed.

'So I asked him what would be a good present, and he told me. So if you don't like it, you can blame him.'

Pearl, puzzled, unwrapped the box. What could her brother have suggested? Then she gasped. 'A smartphone!' It was one of the latest models too, with a touch screen and full internet access . . . 'Wow, Mum! This is amazing!'

'Oh, good.' Linda looked relieved. 'I thought a bear would be more, you know, *personal*, but I guess this will be useful. You can check emails on the go and everything.'

Pearl beamed. 'Thanks, Mum. You're the best.'

Harrison coughed loudly.

'And thanks to you too,' Pearl told him sincerely. 'Honestly, I love it. Great advice!'

Harrison grinned, looking almost like his old, non-grumpy self. 'No problem. Though you'd better not use your netbook password or I might be offended.'

Pearl's jaw dropped. 'How did you . . . ? Did you *hack* into my netbook?'

'Didn't need to,' said Harrison airily. 'You wrote down your password and I found it. So I checked it worked. It was weeks ago.'

'*You used my netbook without asking?*'

Harrison shrugged. 'Don't see why you'd be annoyed. There's nothing on it! You are the least technical person I know.'

Pearl, outraged, turned to her mother. 'Mum!'

'Harrison,' said Linda helplessly, 'you can't just use Pearl's things without asking.'

'I don't go into your room and use your stuff, do I?' complained Pearl.

'Wouldn't care if you did,' said Harrison unconvincingly.

'Oh, really? What about that time I came in and you were hiding something under your bed?' Pearl crossed her arms.

Harrison's eyes widened. 'Don't know what you're talking about,' he said, but he cast a nervous glance at their mother.

'So if Mum decided to go into your room and check under your bed tonight, there wouldn't be anything to find, is that right?' challenged Pearl.

'Kids, kids!' Linda implored, holding up her hands. 'We were having such a nice evening!'

A waiter appeared. 'Can I get you anything else?'

'No thank you,' said Linda, harassed. 'Just the bill, please.'

'Of course, madam.'

Pearl and Harrison glared at each other across the table. There was an awkward silence.

'Normal service is resumed, then,' said Linda, trying to make a joke.

Nobody answered.

♥

By the time Pearl got into bed that night, she was feeling guilty about spoiling the evening with her family. True, Harrison shouldn't have used her netbook without her permission, but she had to admit he was right that there wasn't anything to find. Even her emails were fairly innocuous. Emails made her think of Bailey. She wondered what he was doing at the moment. Schools had broken up, so he'd be on his summer holidays. What did he do in his spare time? she wondered. He loved writing, but what else did he do? Was he into music, football – what? Not for the first time, she wished she'd made up with him earlier after their argument in the park. They could even have gone out on a date or something . . .

The smartphone blinked at her from the bedside table. It was charging up. Pearl had glanced at the manual and given up; it looked far too sophisticated. She hoped it wouldn't be complicated to figure out. She knew she'd find it easier to keep in touch with school friends if she had a phone that could connect to the internet at the touch of a button. Maybe she could even get onto Facebook like everyone else.

Pearl yawned and turned over in bed. The swelling on her cheek had almost completely gone down now, and even the ugly bruise was fading. It was lucky she had such dark skin – it didn't show bruises nearly as easily as white skin. And there were just two days to go before the first day of the competition! Two more sleeps, as her mother used to say . . .

♥

Kat and Lizzie were in disgrace. 'I can't believe you would be so stupid,' fumed Jen. 'Don't the Olympics mean anything to you?'

'Of course they do,' snapped Kat, her face flushed and her eyes bright. 'But we're not robots, you know.'

Lizzie shushed her twin. 'You're not helping,' she muttered.

'What happened?' Pearl asked Hollie-Mae in a whisper. She, Millie and Evie had only just arrived at the gym.

Hollie-Mae drew them aside. 'Kat and Lizzie got caught by security guards climbing over a fence last night,' she said quietly, though the hint of a smile lurked at the corner of her mouth.

Pearl was gobsmacked. '*What?*'

'They were at a party or something in south London,' Hollie-Mae went on. 'With some guys from the basketball team. It sounds like it got a bit out of hand, and the lads suggested they could climb the park fence instead of walking all the way round to the main entrance.'

'But it's electrified!' exclaimed Millie. 'They'd be killed!'

'They didn't get that far,' said Hollie-Mae. 'One of the security guards spotted them on the CCTV and called the police.'

Pearl, Millie and Evie stared, mouths agape. 'They were *arrested*?' gasped Evie.

'No, not Kat and Lizzie,' replied Hollie-Mae. 'Though they did all get taken to the police station. Kat and Lizzie didn't get back to their rooms until three a.m.'

'Are they *crazy*?' asked Evie. 'It's the day before our technical routine!'

'I don't think they quite knew what was happening until it was too late.' Hollie-Mae threw a quick glance over her shoulder to where Jen was still berating the unfortunate twins. 'It sounds like they just got caught up in something. Emily's already had a word, and so's Bonnie. Lizzie's really upset, but Kat keeps saying they didn't do anything wrong and they just wanted to have a laugh. She says she needed to let her hair down after all this serious training. To be honest, I don't think she's helping the situation.'

'What's going to happen?' asked Pearl.

Hollie-Mae shrugged. 'Nothing. They haven't been charged with anything. They're not in official trouble, you know. But they've only had three hours' sleep . . .'

The girls looked at each other in concern. Everyone knew how important it was to re-charge the brain with a decent amount of sleep. Not to mention the down-time for muscles to relax. 'They'll be fine,' said Pearl, trying to sound convinced. 'They're practically the most experienced of all of us.'

'It kind of spoils the atmosphere though, doesn't it?' commented Evie. 'The day before our first routine. We could have done without Emily and Bonnie being annoyed.'

Despite the upset, the team's practice went well and Kat and Lizzie kept their heads down and their brains focused. It was only after lunch that Pearl saw Lizzie stifle a yawn and then glance around in alarm in case anyone was looking. Pearl gave her a small smile, and Lizzie bit her lip and looked away. Pearl couldn't imagine how guilty the two of them must be feeling, but there was no point wishing it hadn't happened. The technical routine was only twenty-four hours away!

♥

When she got back to her room that afternoon, Pearl found an enormous envelope waiting for her in their post locker. In fact, there was quite a pile of envelopes for the girls, and excitedly they took them up to the apartment.

'Cards from my aunts and my grandparents,' said Millie, smiling. 'Oh bless, they found a card with a water baby on it.'

'Ha – I've got the same card!' said Evie with a laugh. 'From my best friend.'

Pearl tore open her huge envelope, wondering who on earth it could be from. 'Oh!' It was a handmade creation, featuring photos of herself and the other girls cut from newspaper and magazine articles. The background was awash with blue and purple tissue paper, and there was a complicated hand-drawn border of Olympic rings. Each girl had a tiny jewelled medal stuck to her chest, and GOOD LUCK was stamped across the middle.

'Wow!' Millie leaned over to look. 'That's amazing – who's it from?'

Pearl opened the card to be confronted with several enormous pages of signatures. In the middle of the first page, someone had written in large letters, 'Go, Pearl and the girls! Wishing you all the luck in the world for the competition! From Lola Cassidy.'

For a moment Pearl stared at the names in confusion, but then she remembered. Of course – the girl at the Kellerman Club! The one who'd done all the interior design. How lovely that she'd gone to so much trouble!

Millie and Evie were poring over the signatures. 'She must have taken this round everyone in Parchester,' said Millie wonderingly. 'There must be hundreds of names here. It's not a card, it's a good luck *book*.'

'Look, there's a whole page from your school,' Evie pointed out.

Pearl squinted. 'Even the head's signed it!' Eagerly, she flicked through the other pages. Some of the names meant nothing to her: Kate Morrell, Simon Ballios, Suki Taylor, Scott Fanshawe, Libby Hannigan, Mari Rosenberg . . .

'Fliss Richards!' cried Millie, pointing at a neatly printed name.

'Who?'

'Fliss Richards! You know – she plays the lead in that new BBC One drama. The one about the girl who's half mermaid. *Emily Windsnap*, that's what it's called.'

'Aw, look at this page,' said Evie. 'It's from a dance school. You can see some of the kids are really little.'

There were neatly written names at the top –

Corinne something, Megan Hirst, Alys, Jackie . . . and then the bottom half of the page had names in childish handwriting: Emma Reynolds, Owen Hirst . . .

Many of the names also had good luck messages scrawled next to them. On some pages the names were crammed in so tightly it was hard to read them. Pearl felt her throat close with emotion. So many people had taken the time to write to wish them good luck!

'This is amazing,' said Millie, and Evie agreed.

'You'll have to bring it to dinner this evening to show the others. They'll be blown away.'

♥

As predicted, Pearl's good luck card cheered everyone up. Even Kat and Lizzie, who had been uncharacteristically quiet all day after their telling-off, beamed from ear to ear when they saw it. Emily Van Hest said firmly, 'Well, that settles it. We've got to bring a medal home to Parchester, haven't we?' and was deafened by the cheers.

All the girls went to their apartments early that night, but Pearl knew it would be ages before she could get to sleep. She, Millie and Evie sat up talking in the lounge, but after a while Millie said she was going to bed to read, and Evie said she wanted a bath, so Pearl fetched her new phone to see if she could figure out how to use it.

Once she'd got started, it wasn't as hard as she'd thought, and within twenty minutes she'd managed to access her emails. Her account was full of messages from her friends wishing her well for the next day – and Pearl's heart gave an extra loud thump as she saw one from Bailey too.

Hi Pearl

It feels like ages since we last saw each other. It's probably not very cool of me to say so, but I've missed you. Your mum's come round once or twice for dinner here, and I feel like a right gooseberry. I don't know if they're going to stay together though. Dad says he thinks your mum is going off him. I can't work out if that's a good thing or a bad thing. She's really nice though. I can't believe I was so wrong about her.

Why am I waffling about them?? It's only because I can't think of the right words to say to wish you luck. I suppose I'm trying to think of something that's different; that isn't what everyone else says. 'Good luck' sounds so boring. Maybe I should come up with one of those ancient curses for the other teams instead. 'May all their goggles be filled with clay' or something. Oh – do you even wear goggles in competitions? No, of course not. 'May they all grow an extra leg' – that would ruin things, wouldn't it?

I'm doing it again – sorry. It's like talking too much when you're nervous. I'm coming tomorrow, you know. I've actually got a ticket. Don't ask me how. If I told you, I'd have to kill you. (No, really. The Mafia was involved.) So I shall actually be THERE, cheering you on – not that you'll see me or hear me. But I'd like you to know that I'm there, and I won't take my eyes off you.

NOW I sound like a stalker. That's not good. But you might as well know that I fully intend to ask you out AGAIN and to carry on doing so until you say yes, even if it's just to shut me up.

Good luck tomorrow. And for the next day, of course. I'll actually be at the final too but I'm not telling you why because it's a surprise.

Good luck. Not that you'll need it because you're totally awesome already (I mean that, I'm in awe of you) but the extra luck is so that you don't slip on the side or something. Oh God! Now I've jinxed everything! Maybe I should delete that bit? Too late, I'm pressing SEND . . .

Your Number One Fan (mwahahaha)

Bailey
(Oh, what the hell) xxx

Pearl wiped tears of laughter from her eyes. That was *exactly* what she needed to defuse the tension of the competition. Bailey always seemed to know the right way to say things. Even the fact that he fancied her didn't seem to cause all the horrible awkwardness you usually got in that kind of situation. *He just makes me smile*, thought Pearl, *and that's good because I'm quite a serious person really*. What with the training and her parents' break-up, there hadn't been much fun or laughter in the last year or so. Bailey was a breath of fresh air; someone who could make her smile just by saying hello.

Still smiling, she tried to type a reply, but the keyboard on the phone was so frustrating! She kept hitting the wrong letter by mistake, and she couldn't work out how to switch off the predictive text. In the end, she had to settle for:

Dear Bailey,
It was great to hear from you! Got new phone driving me crazy but thank you for lovely message. Will look out for you tomorrow!
Px

When the Games are over, she told herself, *I will go on a date with him. I can't wait!*

Then she blinked, surprised at herself. *I just wished away the Olympics for a date with a boy! I must be going mad!*

Chapter 16

what a buzz!

'I can't believe it's the actual day,' Evie said, her face pale. 'I didn't sleep a wink, did you?'

Actually, Pearl had slept very well in the end. She'd read and re-read Bailey's email seven times before falling asleep with a smile on her face. But she could tell her friend needed reassurance. 'Hardly at all,' she agreed.

Everyone looked pale and tense, and there was no banter in the locker rooms as they got ready for their morning practice. 'This is the last time we'll run this routine,' Bonnie told them, even though they already knew, 'so make it a good one.'

The technical routines were scheduled for the afternoon, so there were several hours to endure before they would be able to perform in front of the massive crowds expected at the Aquatics Centre. Pearl had thrown back the curtains that morning and felt relieved that the sun was shining. It seemed like a good omen.

Team GB's practice was over in the blink of an eye, or so it felt to the girls, since every team in the competition needed a slot to practice that morning. It was hard not to watch the other teams practising, but Bonnie was quite strict with them. 'There's no point,' she declared firmly. 'If you think they're brilliant, you'll get depressed, and if you think they're rubbish, you won't try so hard. *You* know what kind of standard you must reach. Each of you is responsible for achieving her best, and only her best.'

The girls nodded, their eyes darting to left and right as they saw members of the Spanish, Russian and Australian teams walking by. Pearl tried not to look, but it was hard when their rivals were so close. Everyone knew that the British team wasn't expected to win a medal. They were good, but other teams were better, and had proved so at the World Championships and other competitions. In a way, Pearl thought, that should take the pressure off, but no one wanted to look bad. Coming last would be humiliating! But perhaps, just perhaps, if they had good luck on the day and performed the best they ever had . . . They'd never beat the Spanish or the Russians, but maybe the bronze medal . . . ?

'Focus,' Bonnie was saying, and Pearl blinked guiltily. 'That's your watchword for today and tomorrow. Don't let anything distract you.' She nodded. 'I'll see you later for the warm-up. Make sure you have a decent lunch and a good rest – conserve your energy.' Then she smiled. 'You're going to do me proud, girls, I know it.'

❤

The noise in the Aquatics Centre was so loud that Pearl was momentarily disorientated. There was the usual swimming-pool sound, full of echoes – but with seventeen thousand people in the seats, chattering and shouting, it was as though the very air was somehow alive. *Focus*, Pearl tried to tell herself as the team waited for their turn, but she couldn't help looking around in wonder. Her mum was there, and Harrison too. And Bailey – somewhere. Her eyes searched the spectator gallery but there was no hope of picking out anyone she knew. It was a mass of colour and movement. Lots of people waved Union Jacks, and there were home-made banners too, though Pearl couldn't read them from this distance. She wished she could see Bailey. The sight of his smiling face would do a lot to calm the churning in her stomach. It gave her a funny feeling to know that he could see her but she couldn't see him.

They were the fourth team to perform, and as they were given their cue, a switch flicked in Pearl's head. Suddenly the noise around her faded to a dull hum. She was sharply aware of her own breathing, her body and the other girls around her. They marched out to the side of the pool in perfect unison, just as they'd done a hundred times before in practice. Counting the silent beats in her head, Pearl's body snapped out the rehearsed motions to get her into the starting pose. Then, right on time, the music began, and she dived into the pool.

Every head turn; every kick; every hand movement was as sharp and clean as it had ever been. Pearl's body knew what to do without her telling it; this was the benefit of months of the 'muscle memory' training that was so important. Her brain was cool and clear, like the water. There were no thoughts of Bailey, of her parents, of medals. There was only the water and the rest of the team, moving as one unit, perfectly in sync.

It was a shock to reach the end pose and hear

the eruption of noise that penetrated her eardrums. For a moment Pearl floundered slightly in the water; it was like emerging from a freezer into the warmth of a summer's day. The crowd was going wild, but she had no idea whether it had been a good performance or not. Mechanically, the girls got out of the pool and lined up on the edge to wave to the spectators. Then the scores appeared – good ones too! – and Pearl could feel the girls on either side of her breathe out in relief. They had done it. They were halfway through. One routine down, one to go.

Back in the locker room, Pearl glanced at the clock and jumped in surprise. Fewer than twenty minutes had passed since they'd left it! She suddenly found that her knees felt wobbly, so she sat down on the bench and breathed out.

'You all right, Pearl?' Jen asked anxiously.

'I'm fine – just . . . you know.' Pearl smiled up at her.

Jen smiled back. 'Yeah, I know.'

Georgie let out a whoop. 'What a buzz!' and it was as though her words were a catalyst to everyone else. The room filled with the noises of relief – laughter, cheers and excited chatter. Then Primrose patted Hollie-Mae on the back, and that prompted a whole load of back-patting until the steward came in to remind them that they had to be out of the locker room in four minutes flat or there would be trouble.

Bonnie and Emily were waiting for them out in the athletes' reception and their beaming smiles said it all. 'Good work,' said Emily with feeling. 'Well done, everyone. That's one of the tightest, cleanest performances you've ever given.'

The team exchanged delighted smiles.

'*But*,' said Emily in a warning tone, 'don't get carried away. There's still tomorrow. You still need to focus – more than ever now. There will be time to celebrate afterwards.'

There was an anxious wait for the rest of the teams to perform, but when the session was over, Pearl was thrilled to see that the British team was in fourth position! 'That's amazing!' she exclaimed. 'I didn't think we'd be higher than fifth!'

'*And*,' said Evie, 'it means that we could be in with a shot at a medal . . . !'

'Don't say it, don't say it!' cried Hollie-Mae, overhearing. 'You'll jinx it!'

The others laughed, but Pearl knew how Hollie-Mae felt. It was almost as though, by talking about it, the magical possibility could disappear. They had done well, but there was more to do, and no one could rest on their laurels yet.

Pearl and Evie went out to find Millie, who had been watching from the gallery. She beamed at them. 'That was brilliant!'

Pearl gave her an extra big hug. She couldn't imagine how difficult it must be for Millie to watch her team-mates perform without her. 'Thanks. We should go get a milkshake or something.'

'Your mum's looking for you,' said Millie. 'And, Evie, your mum's here too somewhere.'

Pearl looked around but there were so many people that it was hard to spot anyone in particular. 'We need to get up a bit higher. I wish I'd told Mum where to wait.' *And Bailey*, she suddenly thought. *Bailey's here too!* Would he have waited?

After several minutes of climbing steps and peering at people, Evie spotted her mum and went off with a yelp of recognition. Then Pearl saw Harrison, and within moments she was enveloped in an enormous hug from her mum. Even Harrison looked cheerful. 'That was amazing!' cried Linda, her arms so tightly around her daughter that Pearl almost couldn't breathe. 'You've come on so much – I couldn't believe that routine!'

'Mum! Air!'

Linda stepped back, grinning. 'Sorry, love. Were you happy with the way it went?'

'Yeah,' said Pearl. 'Yes, everyone's really pleased. Though we've still got to get through tomorrow's free routine.'

'You'll storm it,' stated Harrison. His hands were in his jeans pockets and he was trying to look casual, but his eyes shone. 'Piece of cake.'

'You think?' Pearl smiled at her brother. 'Thanks for coming.'

He shrugged. 'Mum made me.' Pearl laughed, and he grinned in response. 'This place is pretty cool. I'd like to go see some other stuff while I'm here.'

'Have you got tickets?' Pearl asked.

'No – I thought I'd just rock up and see what was going on.'

Pearl laughed again. 'You are impossible! Tickets for most stuff sold out over a year ago!'

Harrison's face fell, but then he rallied. 'Fine. I'll just hang around and see if I can get some auto-graphs.'

'We saw Bailey in the audience,' Linda said, remembering. 'He was sitting in a different bank to us, but he waved. I didn't know he was coming.'

'He emailed me last night,' said Pearl, and blushed.

Her mother looked at her more closely. 'Is there anything you want to tell us?'

Pearl rolled her eyes in embarrassment. 'No.'

Linda smiled. 'OK.'

'Bailey, Edward's son?' asked Harrison, with interest.

'Yes,' said Pearl, hoping to change the subject. 'You didn't come with Edward then?'

Linda pulled a face. 'No-o. He was going to come, but we had a bit of an argument yesterday. We're taking a break – just cooling off for a while.'

'Oh.' Pearl couldn't work out if her mum was upset or pleased about this. 'Are you OK?'

Linda brushed a strand of hair away from her eyes. 'I'm fine. I think we got a bit too intense too quickly.' She smiled at Pearl. 'Just like you said. I should have listened to you right from the start, shouldn't I? My clever girl.' She hesitated. 'I think I saw your father in the crowd too.'

'Really?' Pearl felt her heart give a strange thump. But he had said he would try to come, hadn't he? 'Are you sure?'

Linda shook her head. 'No, not really. I caught sight of him and then he disappeared again. It might not have been him at all.'

Nearly a year ago, Pearl would have said that no

way did she want her father to watch her compete – never again. But now she found herself hoping that he *had* been there. Maybe it was time to talk again? Maybe it was time to let him back into her life?

♥

That evening the whole team had dinner together in the enormous canteen. Jen was emotional; her boyfriend had proposed to her that afternoon, and she was sporting a sparkly ring on a shaky finger. 'I can't believe it,' she kept saying. 'I never expected it in a million years.'

Everyone congratulated her, and Kat voiced what they were all thinking: 'You *are* going to have all of us as bridesmaids, aren't you?'

Jen's face was a picture. 'All of you?' she echoed faintly, looking around at the eight eager faces. Then she smiled. 'Oh, what the heck – why not!'

There was a great cheer. 'I wish I was getting married,' sighed Hollie-Mae. 'It's so romantic.'

This sparked a long, involved conversation about different sorts of weddings. Primrose declared she'd get married abroad on a tropical island because she didn't want her cousins getting drunk and making a scene as they had when her elder sister had got married. Lizzie said she'd want a double wedding with her twin, which Kat thought was the worst idea in the world. 'I'm not getting married,' she said firmly. 'I don't see the point.'

Pearl kept quiet. As soon as everyone had started to talk about weddings, she couldn't help thinking of Bailey, and it made her blush again. Goodness, she wasn't old enough to get married yet! And even if she were, who said that she'd want to marry Bailey? *But he is the right sort of person for me*, she thought silently. *I'm really serious but he makes me laugh, and he's good at listening, and it helps that he thinks I'm pretty* . . . What sort of dress would she have if she were to get married?

'You all right, Pearl?' Millie waved a hand in front of her friend's face. 'You're miles away.'

'I'm fine. Sorry, I was . . . never mind.'

The conversation was interrupted by a man who appeared at the table. 'I don't suppose there's a Pearl here, is there?' he asked, looking doubtful.

Pearl was puzzled. 'Yes, that's me.' She didn't know him – she was sure of that.

The man handed over a long red rose in a cellophane wrapper. 'Some boy gave this to me outside the gates and asked me to give it to you. He was quite persistent, actually.' He grinned. 'Guess you've got an admirer.'

There was a chorus of whistles and 'oohs' from the surrounding tables, and much laughter from the rest of the girls. 'Ooh, Pearl, who's it from?' asked Hollie-Mae.

'There's no message,' Pearl told her, feeling her face flame red-hot. 'I don't know who it's from.' But inside, she was quite certain. There was only one boy who'd take so much trouble. She stood up. 'Excuse me – back in a minute.'

There was a chance Bailey was still outside the athletes' area, waiting for her. Maybe if she ran quickly . . . Pearl barged her way past people, ignoring the cries of 'Hey!' and the annoyed glances. All she wanted, in that one moment, was to see him. Just see his face – see him smile at her. That would be enough.

Gasping, she reached the edge of the Athletes' Village and impatiently made her way through the security checkpoint. The sky was still light but there weren't many people around. Everyone who had come to watch events earlier in the day was heading home, carrying plastic bags with the 2012 logo on them, stuffed with programmes and souvenirs.

Pearl swung round, scanning the area. He must be here – he *must*! Surely he wouldn't just send her a red rose and then go home? He'd know she'd want to come out to see him, wouldn't he?

But there was no cute, smiling black boy leaning against the wall waiting for her. No message, no sign that he had ever been there. Just a man with glasses and a brown jacket standing awkwardly by the path, staring at her vaguely.

Pearl's heart sank. He wasn't here. Had she been mistaken? Maybe the rose hadn't been from Bailey at all! She lifted it to her nose, sniffing. It was real, all right – rich and red, with a velvety scent like expensive perfume.

The man in the brown jacket gave her a grin. 'That's pretty,' he observed, and winked.

Instantly, Pearl was alarmed. Had she made a horrible mistake? Had this man sent the rose to her instead? After all, people did send things to the sportsmen and women they admired. She herself occasionally got cards or letters from the general public, and she knew that Tom Daley had been sent all kinds of weird things as fan mail.

Suddenly awkward and embarrassed, Pearl turned abruptly and went back through security into the safety of the Village. Behind her, she heard the man in the brown jacket laughing, and felt stupid. Bailey must be well on his way home by now. Her fingers tightened on the stem of the rose. If it wasn't from him, she didn't think she wanted it.

♥

'You all right?' asked Millie as they headed back to their apartment. 'You look kind of pale.'

Pearl held out the rose. 'You have it.'

'Why? Don't you want it? Pearl . . .' Millie grabbed her arm. 'Talk to me. What's the matter?'

Pearl shook her head. 'I just feel stupid, that's all. I thought that rose was from . . . well, never mind – I was wrong. He wasn't there.'

'Pearl, you're not making any sense.' Millie looked worried. 'We need to talk about this upstairs.'

Millie, Evie and Pearl said goodnight to the other girls and got out of the lift at their floor. Evie was yawning. 'I hope I sleep better tonight. Only one more day to go – I can't believe it.'

But Millie wasn't going to let things go that easily. She tugged Pearl towards the sofa in the little lounge. 'Come on, you have to tell me. What's up?'

Evie stared curiously. 'What's the matter?'

Millie waved the rose at her. 'Pearl's gone all weird over this rose.'

'Really? Why?' Evie sat down with them.

Pearl sighed. 'It's nothing, honestly. I just – I thought it was from Bailey, that's all.'

'Bailey?' asked Millie. 'Why did you think it was from him? I thought you were hardly in touch.'

'He sort of asked me out in an email,' Pearl explained, feeling her face redden.

The other two squealed and immediately demanded details, so much so that Pearl was forced to show them the email on her phone. 'He sounds completely adorable,' sighed Millie after reading it.

'But what makes you think the rose isn't from him?' asked Evie. 'I mean, it would make sense.'

'There's no message with it,' Pearl told her. 'No note. And when I went out to look for him, he wasn't there. And – there was this really weird guy standing there looking at me and *winking* . . .'

'Ohhh . . .' said Millie, understanding. 'I get it. You think maybe it was from him?'

'Well, why would Bailey send me a rose and then not wait for me to come and find him?'

'He knows how busy you are,' said Evie reasonably.

'He probably didn't imagine you'd come running out to look for him. He wouldn't know whether you were eating or sleeping or training or what. You might have been in a meeting. How long's he supposed to wait?'

'You think?'

'Completely,' agreed Millie. 'I mean, put yourself in his shoes. He's got you this rose. He doesn't know how to get it to you, so he gives it to some guy who's coming into the Village. He's got no guarantee that the rose will actually reach you. For all he knows, the messenger might have nicked it to give to his own girlfriend, or dumped it in the nearest bin.'

'*And*,' added Evie, suddenly thinking of a new idea, 'how do you know that the guy who passed you the rose had only just got it? I mean, he might have had it for half an hour before he came to find you. Bailey couldn't hang around outside for too long. They've got CCTV, you know. Some security guard would probably think he was acting suspiciously.'

'What about the weird guy I saw?' asked Pearl obstinately. 'The one who winked at me.'

'Did he actually *say* he'd sent the rose?' demanded Millie.

'No . . .'

'So maybe he was just winking at you because he thought you were pretty,' said Evie. 'And 'cos you were standing there looking helpless.'

Pearl stared at the floor. 'Oh. You think?'

'We don't know for sure,' Millie told her gently, 'but you can't just go jumping to conclusions like that. The most likely thing is that the rose *is* from Bailey. Specially after he sent you that lovely message.'

'You know the simplest way to find out, don't you?' said Evie with a shrug. 'Ask him.'

'Yes!' Millie sat up, her eyes bright. 'Email him now and ask!'

'He won't be home,' Pearl pointed out. 'He probably won't check his emails till tomorrow.'

'He will if he's got a smartphone,' argued Evie. 'He could check them on the train. Ha!'

Pearl looked at her phone. 'What if I ask him and he says it's not from him?'

Evie rolled her eyes in exasperation. 'You are hopeless, Pearl! At least you'll *know*, won't you? Good grief!'

'Evie . . .' said Millie. 'It's a boy and he's kind of cute. Don't be mean.'

Evie held up her hands. 'All right, all right. I think

it's sweet, I really do.' She got up. 'I'm going to bed. Let me know what happens in the morning.' She grinned at Pearl and left the room.

Millie stood up. 'I'm off too. You don't need me peering over your shoulder.'

'What should I say?'

Millie smiled. 'I'm sure you'll think of something. Give us a hug.'

♥

When she was alone, Pearl opened a new email to Bailey. She stared at the screen for a long time before she wrote:

Hi Bailey

How are you? What did you think of the routine today? We were all pretty happy with the way things went, and our coach says we're in a good position for tomorrow's free programme. I was sorry not to see you after the competition. My mum and Harrison came and we all met up outside the Aquatics Centre afterwards. They didn't stay long. The whole team had dinner together in the canteen and now we're all off for an early night.

Oh – someone sent me a beautiful red rose! Do
you know who it was from? ;-)
Pearl

She hesitated. Had she worded it the right way? If Bailey hadn't sent the rose, would he be worried that she had another admirer? Or would it make him feel bad for *not* sending her something?

Pearl sighed. It was all so hard! She clicked 'send' and put the phone down beside her. Outside, the sky was finally darkening, though there were too many streetlights to be able to see the stars. She got up and went to the window. London was so big – as far as you could see, and miles beyond. Houses, streets, cars, flats, offices . . . and people, in their hundreds of thousands.

Suddenly she felt a wave of homesickness. Parchester wasn't a small place but it was tiny compared with London. And it was *familiar*. Whenever she'd been away before she'd always had this moment where she remembered everyone and everything back home and wished she were there.

But it wouldn't be long now. Tomorrow was their last day of the competition, and then it would all be over. They'd move out, go home, start training for the next competition . . . but there would never be another London Olympics. They all knew that their chance of a medal was small, but Pearl couldn't help hoping.

She looked up at the sky and could just make out one tiny twinkling star. She wished as hard as she could that they wouldn't be going home empty-handed.

Chapter 17

could anything ever be so amazing again?

Emily smiled at them all. 'I just wanted to say thank you. It's not something we say to you often, but we do appreciate the hours and hours you all put into training and practising. Each and every one of you has given a hundred per cent, and I know how much you've had to sacrifice in order to do this. Of course, you're all so lucky that you're *able* to devote so much to a sport that you adore, but there will always be times when it's a slog rather than a joy. At those times, a person's true mettle shines through. You've all been through tough times in order to make it, and I hope you'll agree that it's worth it. To be here, competing in the Olympics in our own capital city, is a huge honour. Only a tiny fraction of people will be able to say, "I was there," and regardless of

247

how we do today, I want you to know that I am proud of you. It's been a long journey but we're here, and so now let's make the most of it.' She beamed. 'This is the last time you'll perform this routine, and it's the only time it matters. Go out there, enjoy it and make us proud.'

Pearl found there were tears in her eyes by the time Emily had finished. But there was also a great swell of pride in her heart, and she thought to herself, *Yes! This is me, this is my life, this is what I love! And I am the luckiest girl in the world to be able to do it!* She was pleased to see Emily give Millie a special hug. Poor Millie, who had to watch from the sidelines, knowing that she had come *this* close to taking part herself. She waited for her friend as the other girls went to change.

'Don't get left behind,' Millie said, though there were tears in her eyes too. She gave Pearl a watery smile. 'Have a great swim, Pearl. You know I'll be cheering you on.'

Pearl reached out and gave her a giant squeeze. 'Love you, Mills.'

'Love you too.'

Pearl's heart was pounding as she walked into the locker room, but as soon as she stepped into her costume, a strange calm swept over her. The outside world faded away and there was only herself and the rest of her team, checking makeup, smoothing down hair with an extra slick of gel, snapping the elastic straps against their shoulders. No one spoke; they didn't need to. Everyone had their own way of getting focused. Pearl went through the ritual of changing – taking off her right sock before her left; smoothing back her hair before pulling on her costume; rolling her clothes into a tight ball. The familiarity was soothing.

She knew her mum and Harrison wouldn't be there today. They simply hadn't been able to get tickets, even though Linda had tried all the ways she knew how. As for Bailey – he'd sent a very cryptic late-night email:

Hi Pearl
A rose, eh? Can't imagine who would send you that . . . ;-) Thought you were brilliant. Got a surprise for you tomorrow!
Bx

Pearl had pondered over the 'surprise' all morning. What could it be? She checked the post locker before she left after lunch, but there was nothing from Bailey. Was he going to get a message

to her somehow? He said he was going to be here –
would he come and find her after the competition
was over? There would be no chance of spotting him
among the thousands of spectators.

She wasn't wondering any more, though. Pearl's
mind was cool, calm and focused as she lined up with
the other girls. The cue came, and they marched out
in perfect unison, as always. The noise from the home
crowd was almost painful, but Pearl tuned it out as
she had been taught.

They took up their positions, and the music
began.

Afterwards, Pearl didn't know how well it had
gone. In some strange way it was as though she
had split into two – one body performing the
moves with mechanical precision; the other floating
above the water and watching it all with detached
interest. The water, the music – it all fused together
into an almost spiritual experience, so that when the
last beat sounded, Pearl found herself beaming at
the crowd through a haze of tears. Her whole body
tingled with joy. Could anything ever be so amazing
again?

They swam to the side and took their places,
waiting for the scores. And the scores were *good*! Pearl
didn't dare turn her head to see the others' reactions,

but she knew they must feel as excited as she did. There were still three teams to swim, but their combined score put them in first place! So they hadn't dropped a place since yesterday – and there was still a tiny chance . . .

The girls exchanged anxious glances as they filed out. There was to be no changing out of their costumes; instead, they pulled on tops and tracksuit trousers to keep warm. The medal ceremony was to follow on as soon as the last team had swum. 'At least we won't have to wait long,' Pearl whispered to Evie, who nodded, her face pale and tense. In only a few minutes they would know whether they had done enough for a medal.

Three teams remained to swim: China, Russia and Spain. After the technical programme, the top two places had gone to Spain and Russia. The Chinese team had to swim their free programme next. The Team GB girls knew that their own score was unlikely to be good enough to beat Russia or Spain, so if they had any chance at all of a medal, it would be the bronze. And so everything hung on China's performance right now.

Pearl held her breath as the eight girls leaped into the water and began their routine. They were so good! There was no hint of an error between them. Their arms and legs snapped up and out in perfect synchronicity, and their two throw-lifts were superb. Pearl wondered if, just sometimes, one or two girls were a little ahead of the music, but it was so hard to tell from where they were sitting. She knew the judges would have a much better view.

The routine ended with a climactic sequence of kicking legs and spinning bodies, and the crowd erupted into applause. Pearl's heart sank. They were too good, she knew it. There would be no chance of a medal for the British team now, not after that. What a dreadful, depressing shame!

The Chinese girls, petite and beautiful, lined up to receive their marks. Pearl glanced along the side of the pool, where the Russians were waiting to come on. There might be a battle for gold, she supposed, if the Russians had a fantastic free programme. The Spanish would have to pull everything out of the bag to stay in the top spot . . .

She jumped as the two girls on either side of her suddenly leaped to their feet. 'YES!' cried Jen, punching the air.

'I can't believe it!' Georgie was saying.

Pearl looked around, baffled. What had she missed? Then she looked up at the scoreboard . . .

China hadn't beaten them! Their scores were good, but at the bottom, unmistakably, was the number two next to the ranking. That meant that Team GB were still ranking number one with only two teams left to swim!

Pearl's mouth dropped open. 'No!' she breathed. 'It can't be!'

The rest of the girls were beside themselves with excitement. 'We're getting a medal, we're getting a medal!' cried Primrose. She hugged Evie, who reached out to Kat, who pulled in Lizzie – and within seconds, all eight girls were in a massive group hug, jumping up and down and screaming.

'Girls, girls!' shouted Bonnie and Emily. 'You have to calm down! The next team is ready to swim!'

Sure enough, the music for the Russian team was just beginning. Reluctantly, the girls sat down again. Pearl's heart was beating so fast she thought it might burst out of her chest. A medal! A real Olympic medal! She'd dreamed about it, of course, but now that it was actually going to happen . . . it still felt like a dream!

'If the Russians or Spanish mess up, then we might even get silver,' whispered Primrose.

Pearl's eyes widened. Silver! Surely not! She watched the team in the water, not daring to blink in case she missed a tiny error. The Russians were good – very good – but then she'd been wrong about China, hadn't she?

There was no mistake this time. The Russians took top ranking, with only the Spanish team left to compete. Unless all eight girls suddenly took leave of their senses, Spain would certainly get gold or silver, which left the bronze for Team GB. Pearl felt a tiny twinge of disappointment and almost laughed out loud. Disappointed that they were only going to be third! It was a ridiculous feeling, given that they had expected to go home empty-handed!

The British girls sat side by side, hand in hand, and watched the final performance. It was brilliant, with moves that made them gasp in admiration. 'We *so* have to learn to do that one,' murmured Primrose after a particularly spectacular combined lift. There was no question that the Spanish team had outdone themselves, and the marks reflected that – a clear gold medal by quite a margin. The Spanish girls whooped and cheered at the results, several of them bursting into tears.

The final result had been decided. The gold medal went to Spain, the silver to Russia and the bronze to Great Britain. One by one, the teams were announced, and the Spanish national anthem echoed around the Aquatics Centre.

Taking her place on the podium alongside her eight team-mates was the proudest moment of Pearl's life. She couldn't wipe the smile off her face. Her cheek muscles ached, and still she felt as though the joy was bursting out of her like the sun. Her fingers were clenched around the medal that hung from her neck, as though by gripping it so hard she could prove to herself it was really real. Up on the scoreboard, their names were listed in lights for all to see:

ELIZABETH BENSON-ROWE

KATHERINE BENSON-ROWE

PRIMROSE CAYLEY

GEORGINA HARRISON

EVELYN IVORY

PEARL OKEKE

JENNIFER SUGDEN

HOLLIE-MAE WEBB

RESERVE: MILLIE EDWARDS

Pearl was so pleased that Millie was entitled to a

medal too, even though she hadn't swum. It made her happiness that much greater to see her best friend beaming alongside. They waved and smiled and laughed and had their photos taken – and then, suddenly, it was over. Back to get changed and leave the Olympic pool that had dominated their lives for over a year. Back to normal training, and preparation for the next competition. But Pearl knew there would never be another competition like this one. As they left the poolside, she took one last look back, trying to fix the sight in her memory for ever.

Emily and Bonnie came into the locker room and hugged them all. 'Amazing,' Bonnie kept saying. 'Good job!' Pearl had never seen the two of them look so happy.

'Get changed quickly,' Emily told them, 'but don't take off all your makeup. There are some journalists waiting outside who want interviews. I've got a list here of which of you has been allocated to each journalist.' She turned to Pearl. 'Pearl, as the youngest, you've been specially requested by CBBC.'

Pearl was taken aback. 'Me, on CBBC?'

'Yes, they're doing a special feature on the Olympics. Is that all right?'

Evie giggled. 'You'll probably be interviewed by Bob the Builder.'

Pearl grinned. 'That sounds fun. I'm up for it!'

'Excellent.' Emily smiled at her. 'I'm very proud of you, Pearl. I'm proud of everyone, of course, but you've coped particularly well, given your age. You haven't let all this go to your head, and I feel you've really matured over the past few months.'

'Thanks, Emily.' Pearl felt a bit embarrassed that she was saying all this in front of the other girls.

Emily nodded. 'Right, then – see you all outside, when I'll tell you where to go and who to speak to.'

♥

Most of the interviews were to take place in the Press Building, but Pearl was told that the CBBC interview would be held in a quiet spot outside the Aquatics Centre. Bonnie pointed to where a cameraman was standing alongside a girl holding a sound boom and a couple of other people chatting over a clipboard, and Pearl quickly headed across, hoping her hair didn't look too greasy in the sunlight. That was the trouble with the

257

gel they used; it was perfect for keeping hair in place underwater but it looked horrible out of the pool!

She caught her breath as she neared the little group. The two people talking over the clipboard – one of them was tall and wore glasses, but the other . . . it looked almost like . . . but that was impossible . . .

'Bailey!'

He turned, his face breaking into a huge smile. 'There you are! Congratulations!'

'Thank you!' Seeing his face made her feel warm inside, but Pearl was bewildered. What was Bailey doing with a team from CBBC?

The tall man stepped forward and held out his hand for Pearl to shake. He was holding the clipboard. 'Hi, Pearl. Thanks so much for coming to talk to us. I'm Paul, the director, and that's Gavin with the camera and Luisa with the boom. I gather you and Bailey are old friends.'

'Yes, but . . .' Pearl was speechless. 'I didn't know he was . . . um . . .'

'I won another competition,' Bailey told her. 'Through the *Youth Voice* magazine. They told me about the CBBC competition to report on the Olympics. I had to write an essay about why I wanted to do it and which sport I was interested in. So I wrote about synchro, of course.' He grinned again. 'Simples.'

'Wow.' Suddenly Pearl felt shy. Bailey could have picked any sport he liked to report on. With his talent for words, she was sure he must have won easily. He could have been interviewing Usain Bolt, or Chris Hoy, or Rebecca Adlington, or Tom Daley ... but he wasn't. He'd chosen to interview her!

'OK,' said Paul, becoming practical. 'If you can stand over here, Pearl – and Bailey, you stand there ...' He moved them into position. 'Bailey, you've got your questions all ready, haven't you?'

'Yes,' said Bailey, 'but I might throw in one or two extras, if that's all right.'

Paul nodded. 'That's fine. A good interviewer will listen carefully to the answers and make sure the next question follows on naturally. Don't worry if you don't manage to get through everything on your list. The important thing is that we get a good idea of what it's all been like for Pearl.' He turned towards her. 'Is there anything you want to ask, or shall we just go for a take?'

'Um ...'

'Don't worry about fluffing your answers or

anything,' Paul assured her. 'We don't have to do it all in one take. If you make a mistake or you want to go back and answer something again, we can easily do that and edit it all together. Just be as relaxed as you can.'

'OK.' Pearl was perfectly certain she couldn't be at all relaxed, not with a TV camera in her face and a possible future boyfriend standing next to her! But she took a few deep breaths, like she did before a performance, and tried to look as much like her usual self as possible.

Paul nodded at Gavin and Luisa. 'You two all set?'

'Yup.' Luisa lowered the boom until it was just above Pearl and Bailey's heads.

Gavin nodded too, his eyes fixed on the camera viewer. 'Rolling.'

'Excellent,' said Paul. 'Off you go then, Bailey.'

Bailey looked straight into the camera. 'Hi there, I'm Bailey Ross, and today I'm outside the Olympic Aquatics Centre with Pearl Okeke. Pearl is the youngest member of the British Synchronized Swimming Team, and they have just won a bronze medal!' He turned to Pearl. 'Congratulations, Pearl!'

'Thank you,' Pearl replied, trying not to be hyper-aware of the black camera lens pointing at her. 'We're really – well, we're—' *Oh no, I'm sounding like a moron.*

'Over the moon, I bet,' interrupted Bailey.

Pearl threw him a grateful look. 'Yeah, completely. It still seems like a dream.' She fingered the medal around her neck.

'Can you hold it up for the camera?' Bailey asked.

Pearl did so, feeling a bit silly.

'I bet you'll never want to take it off,' went on Bailey. 'What is it about the Olympics that makes a medal from the Games more special than any other?'

'I don't know,' Pearl answered. 'I was thinking exactly that the other day. I mean, we compete all year in different competitions, and I suppose for us the biggest is the World Swimming Championships – but the Olympics, well . . . That only happens every four years, so that makes it special, and also they have such a history, you know, going back centuries. Everyone's heard of the Olympic Games.'

Bailey was nodding, as though she was giving the best possible answer, so Pearl felt slightly less awkward. He grinned at her now. 'And are you disappointed that you didn't get gold or silver?'

'Are you kidding?' Pearl asked. 'We never thought we'd get any kind of medal at all!' She blushed. 'I probably shouldn't say that.'

Bailey laughed.

'What I mean is, it's taken us a long time to improve our rankings,' Pearl said. 'Last year at the Worlds, we came ninth, which was great for us. But we've never made the top three before, so this is really special. To get a bronze medal . . .' She shook her head. 'It means the world to us.'

'How will you be celebrating?' asked Bailey.

'I haven't really thought about it yet. It's our last night in the Athletes' Village tonight, so I expect the team will go out for a meal together. Then maybe I'll do something special when I get home tomorrow.'

'You've been here for a couple of weeks now, haven't you?' asked Bailey. 'What have you missed most about home?'

'Um . . .' Pearl thought for a minute. 'My mum and my brother, of course. And I haven't seen my school friends for ages because I've been training so hard.'

'Anyone else?' prompted Bailey, a slight twinkle in his eye.

Pearl hesitated. *Does he mean what I think he means?* 'There is someone I'm looking forward to seeing, yes.'

'Someone special?' suggested Bailey.

Behind the camera, Pearl could see Paul glancing down at his clipboard in surprise. She guessed these questions weren't on the list! 'He could be special, yes,' she admitted, feeling her face start to heat up. Surely Bailey wouldn't embarrass her on national television?

'Whoever he is, he sounds like a lucky guy,' said Bailey, grinning. 'I bet he can't wait to hear from you.'

'Well,' said Pearl carefully, 'I expect I'll be able to see him at the weekend.'

Bailey's grin widened. 'He'll be watching his inbox, waiting for a time and place.' He turned back to face the camera. 'Thanks so much to Pearl Okeke for talking to me, and congratulations again to the British Synchro team for their bronze medals. This is Bailey Ross, reporting for CBBC.'

'And . . . cut,' said Paul, stepping forward. 'That was great, guys, thank you.' His gaze flicked from one to the other. 'Of course, we got slightly off track towards the end there . . .'

'Did we?' said Bailey innocently. 'Sorry about that.'

'It was . . . interesting,' said Paul. He looked as though he wanted to say more, but then changed his mind. 'Well, I'll watch it back and see how it comes across. It might be edited for the broadcast later.'

'No problem,' said Pearl. She suddenly felt a great desire to giggle. This was turning into such a surreal day! First the team won an Olympic medal, and now she was being interviewed on television by the boy who fancied her! Could things get any weirder? She caught Bailey's eye, which was a big mistake because he was trying not to laugh too. Pearl pressed her lips together as tightly as she could to prevent the laughter bubbling out.

'Right,' said Paul, who had been consulting with Gavin, the cameraman. 'That's all we need. We've got to get this straight to the Press Centre so that it can go out in this evening's bulletin.' He shook Pearl's hand. 'Thanks again, Pearl – and many congratulations.'

'Thank you.'

'Bailey, if you come back with me, I'll show you how we do the editing.'

Bailey's face fell slightly. 'Oh – oh yes, of course.'

Pearl too felt disappointed. She'd been hoping Bailey would be able to stay around for a few minutes. They could chat, and – and – well, who knew? But instead she had to wave him off, wishing that the weekend would hurry up so that she could finally spend some time with him . . .

♥

Pearl was on her way back to the Village when she heard a man call her name. To her astonishment, her dad came puffing up to her. 'Dad! What are you doing here?'

Winston was beaming all over his face. 'Came to see you swim, didn't I?'

'You mean – you were there, in the Aquatics Centre?'

He nodded. 'Yup. Thought you were absolutely brilliant, love.' He hesitated for a moment. It was clear he wanted to step forward and hug her but wasn't sure how it would be received.

Pearl's head felt like it was upside-down in the pool again. All these things happening one after the other – she wasn't sure she could cope! 'Thanks, Dad. It was really nice of you to come.'

'Are you sure?' He looked at her nervously. 'I didn't know if you'd be pleased or not. I know we've got a lot of stuff to sort out still.'

'Yeah . . .' Pearl agreed. 'But I *am* pleased you came, honest, Dad. I think . . . I think maybe I got some things wrong in the past. I mean, maybe I was a bit too hard on you.'

He smiled. 'You don't have to apologize, love. It wasn't your fault.'

'No, but maybe it wasn't as much *your* fault as I thought it was.' Pearl shook her head. 'Everything just got kind of messed up.'

'I know.'

'But I'm glad you came. Mum couldn't get tickets for today, so it's nice to have – to have one member of my family there.'

Her dad looked embarrassed but pleased. 'I'd like to see a bit more of you and Harrison,' he said. 'You know – take you out for the day or something, every now and then.'

'I'd like that,' said Pearl. 'I really would.'

He smiled at her again. 'It's great to see you, Pearl. You look so grown up. I can't believe I've got an Olympic medallist as a daughter! I'm so proud of you!'

Before she could move, he leaned in to give her a quick hug. 'Can't help it,' he said apologetically. 'I feel like I want to tell everyone walking past that you're my daughter.'

His pride made Pearl glow. *I have missed him*, she thought with a twinge of sadness. *We'll never get that time back. But maybe we can start to make up for it now.*

Winston glanced towards the Athletes' Village. 'You going back to change?'

'Yeah. Got to take all this stuff off my face and wash my hair.'

'Can I – can I walk you to the gate?'

'Course.' She shot him a look. 'But only if you promise not to stop everyone we pass to tell them I'm your daughter.'

He laughed. 'I promise.'

Chapter 18

you're extraordinary

'Maybe it would look better on the other wall?' said Linda, staring hard at Pearl's beautiful bronze medal, which was hanging from a hook over the fireplace. 'I think the light's better there.'

Pearl laughed. 'You've tried it in about four different places already, Mum.'

'I know, I know. But it's got to be right.'

'I think you need a second hook,' said Harrison unexpectedly. 'To spread out the ribbon. So it's not just hanging straight down.'

Linda looked puzzled. 'What do you mean?'

'Look.' He showed her. 'So that the ribbon hangs over two hooks, not one, and it makes a triangle shape. It shows off the medal better.'

Pearl laughed. 'You're as bad as each other.'

Harrison grinned. 'If I've got a famous sister, I'm going to milk it as much as possible.'

Pearl grinned back. 'It won't help you get girlfriends.'

'Don't need it to.' Harrison stuck out his tongue. 'Already got Malaika.' They both laughed.

It was amazing how the atmosphere had changed since Pearl had returned. Only a couple of days had passed, but the house felt lighter somehow, as though a heavy burden had been lifted. Pearl wasn't quite sure what exactly had happened. Was it the fact that Dad was now back in their lives? Was it the fact that Mum seemed happier, even though she'd decided to break up with Edward? Or was it simply that she herself felt she had finally been able to step off the Olympic treadmill and take a much-needed break?

Whatever the reasons, Pearl decided, it was definitely better this way. Mum had even said to her, 'You should go out with your friends at the weekends. You shouldn't be stuck at home with me. You've got your own life to lead.'

Pearl had been taken aback. 'Are you sure, Mum? I mean, you've always said how much you like spending time with me, and all that mother-and-daughter stuff . . .'

Her mum smiled. 'And I do like spending time with you. I always will. But I've been selfish, keeping you to myself all the time. At your age, friends are so important. You should make time for them.'

'Won't you be lonely?' asked Pearl.

Linda sighed. 'You know, I think it's about time I learned how to be on my own sometimes. I need to stop depending on other people to make me happy. People need their own space, including me. I just have to learn how to enjoy it a bit more.' She looked shy for a moment. 'I've signed up for a yoga class at that health club, Kellerman's. I met the woman who runs it in a coffee shop in Parchester the other day, and she said I could try a class for free.'

'That's a great idea!' said Pearl. 'We use yoga sometimes in training. I think it's brilliant.'

'Well, we'll see,' said her mum. But she looked happier than Pearl had seen her in over a year.

True to her word, Linda had insisted that Pearl should go out with her friends on Saturday night. 'Oh, you don't want me hanging around,' she said, when Pearl had tried to suggest that she come along too. 'Go out with your friends – be a teenager.'

Several of Pearl's friends had emailed and rung her excitedly, congratulating her on her success and asking her if she was going to be in town this weekend. Some of the synchro team were going to be around too. But Pearl knew there was only one person she was really desperate to see.

Linda had recorded the CBBC interview for her daughter, since it had gone out only a couple of hours after it had taken place. As expected, the bit towards the end, where Bailey had asked about 'someone special', had been edited out. It made Pearl smile to watch it, remembering the bit that no one would ever see. Watching Bailey's face on screen did funny things to her tummy, and she ran the short interview back so that she could see it twice more. She wished she could have thought of something cleverer to say, but at least it wasn't as bad as the first time Bailey had interviewed her!

She'd emailed him as soon as she could, suggesting a place and time to meet, and giving him her phone number at last. He'd agreed immediately, and now she was sitting on a bus, wearing smart clothes that felt very unfamiliar after the weeks of tracksuits and swimming costumes, along with a light dusting of the Bobbi Brown powder she'd bought the day of the makeover.

It was a warm evening and the sky was still very light. The bus was full too – everyone seemed to be heading into Parchester for an evening out. Pearl tried to remember the last time she'd been into town on a

Saturday night, and failed. Surely not for a long time – not since before her father had left. It was a wonder her school friends were still keen to meet up with her. She felt ashamed for abandoning them over the past year. She hadn't meant to, but what with training so hard with the team, there hadn't been much time for old friends. *There will be now*, she told herself, and felt good about it. Training would pick up again, of course, but for a few weeks at least she would have more time to herself.

However, her friends would have to wait a little longer, because she had arranged to meet Bailey first and she didn't want to have to share him just yet. The bus swung onto the High Street, and Pearl pressed the bell for the next stop.

Her heart hammered as she made her way down the steps and off the bus. Millie and Evie had given her so much advice about her first date: 'Don't make too much of an effort,' Millie had said, 'otherwise you'll come across as fake.'

'No,' disagreed Evie, 'she should make sure she looks absolutely amazing so that he knows how lucky he is to be going out with her.'

In the end, Pearl had had to ask them not to give her any more advice because it made her head hurt!

She walked down the street and into the

pedestrianized shopping area. They were due to meet outside Coffee Republic, and as Pearl rounded the corner, she saw him. Bailey had his hands jammed into his pockets and was scanning the area, looking slightly uncomfortable. Within seconds, he'd seen her. Pearl took a deep breath and headed over.

She'd imagined this meeting so many times over the last twenty-four hours that it all felt slightly surreal, as though it wasn't really happening. 'Hi,' she said.

'Hi,' said Bailey. For a moment she thought he was going to lean forward to kiss her cheek, but he obviously thought better of it. 'You OK?'

'Yeah. You?'

'Yeah.'

It was strange, Pearl thought, how going on an official date made everything awkward. She and Bailey had chatted so easily on previous occasions, and over the internet – how come, now that they were actually supposed to be getting to know each other, she couldn't think of a single thing to say?

'You want a coffee?' asked Bailey, gesturing towards the shop.

Pearl hesitated. 'Not really. I wondered – what about the ice-cream place?'

He broke into a grin. 'Now *that's* a great idea.'

And suddenly the awkwardness had gone. As they

headed for Iced Wonders, Pearl told Bailey about the morning after the competition, when they'd all had to pack up their bags and everyone had got very emotional. 'It was kind of a relief when we got back to Parchester,' she admitted. 'I mean, I love them all, but we spend so much time together it can get kind of intense, you know?'

Bailey nodded. 'Have you got a bit of a break now?'

'Yes – two whole weeks! Then back into training for the next competition. And I want to take some exams, so I've got to talk to the school about catching up.'

'Will the swim people let you off to go to school?'

'They have to. The Olympics was a special case. Besides, even though I want to do synchro for ages to come, I will need some qualifications too. Now's a good time to do them.'

Bailey laughed. 'Not many people would be looking forward to going back to school.'

'I would stay in the pool all the time if I could,' admitted Pearl, 'but I can do that in a couple of years when I've done my exams. There's loads of time. Jen's twenty-seven and she's still competing. Hopefully I might even make another Olympics!'

'Win the gold next time,' suggested Bailey, and Pearl laughed.

'Yeah, aim high.'

'Well, for now I'm aiming at ice cream,' said Bailey.

They studied the various types through the glass. 'Honeycomb,' said Pearl. 'Strawberry and white chocolate, mmm . . .'

'It has to be double choc-chip brownie for me,' said Bailey decisively. 'No contest.'

Pearl smiled. 'I thought girls were supposed to be the ones who were obsessed with chocolate?'

'Who says I'm obsessed?' Bailey challenged. 'I don't eat it *all* the time, you know. Just once or twice a day.' He grinned.

Pearl eventually chose a scoop of coffee and a scoop of vanilla choc cookie, and they sat down in the window to eat.

'Does this feel kind of weird?' asked Bailey.

Pearl let out a thankful breath. 'Yeah, it does. I mean, we've seen each other lots of times before, but now we're on an actual date, it feels odd, like it's harder to talk about things.'

There was a slight pause. 'I meant did it feel weird being back in Parchester after all that time at the Olympics,' said Bailey slowly.

Pearl felt herself go cold. *How totally embarrassing!* 'Oh. Oh, right.' She concentrated on her ice cream, unable to look up at him.

'You're right though,' said Bailey after another pause. 'It does feel weird being on a date. Like, together. Even though I've – I've thought about it a lot.'

'Have you?' Pearl asked, still not looking at him.

Bailey shrugged. 'Quite a bit.'

'So . . .' She spooned out the last bit of ice cream. 'What do we do now?'

'Um – did you want any more?'

'No, I'm fine, thanks.'

Bailey finished his ice cream hastily. 'Then I guess we could go . . . for a walk, or something.'

'OK.' She stood up.

They headed out. Pearl felt as though every nerve in her body was jangling. It was halfway between excitement and fear, as though she knew something was coming but wasn't sure whether she'd like it. As they walked, Bailey reached for her hand and held it. She glanced at him and he smiled at her. *I don't know what to do next!* she thought with a faint feeling of panic. *Should I say something, or – or try to kiss him – or what? Do I want to kiss him right now? Would it be better to wait for exactly the right moment, or is it better to get it out of the way?*

They walked down the street together, Pearl's brain chuntering frantically. Bailey didn't say anything, and she wondered if he was waiting for her to make some kind of move. *But what?* Suddenly, competing in the Olympics no longer felt like the most nerve-racking moment of her life.

Bailey stopped outside a shop window. Inside were several shelves of Olympic souvenirs – Union Jack tea towels, bunting, porcelain plates, mugs with the 2012 logo, key rings . . . 'Do you think,' he said, 'that if we go in and you show them your medal, they'd let you have something for free?'

Pearl looked at him, startled, but he had a mischievous smile. 'I didn't bring my medal,' she said.

'Foiled!' cried Bailey.

He looked so cute and happy that, without thinking, Pearl leaned forward and kissed him on the cheek.

Instantly, he turned to look at her, surprised. Pearl too felt surprised. *I didn't mean to do that!* ran through her head.

'Um . . .' he said.

Pearl glanced around, blushing. There were still quite a lot of people around, sitting in outside cafés, chatting on the benches, strolling along looking in windows. It wasn't exactly a private location for this kind of thing! 'Sorry,' she said quickly, turning away from him.

His grip on her hand tightened. 'Are you kidding?

Don't say sorry! Unless . . .' His eyes darkened. 'Unless you didn't mean . . .'

'Come on,' said Pearl, wishing more and more that the ground would open up under her feet. 'I just don't think this is the right place.'

'Oh. Oh, right.' He allowed her to pull him along.

Pearl was thinking, *Help! I don't want to have my first proper kiss in public! But where on earth can we go?*

At the end of the street there was a choice of left or right. Pearl looked desperately both ways.

'Over the road.' Bailey pointed. There was a children's playground set back from the street, partially hidden by trees, and at this time of the evening, with the light finally starting to fade, it was empty.

'All right.'

They crossed the road at the lights, and Bailey held open the playground gate for Pearl. 'Swings!' she said in delight.

Bailey gave a mock groan. 'No way! They make me feel sick!'

'You big baby.' She settled on a swing and pushed off from the ground. 'I love them!'

Bailey sat down carefully on the next swing and swung half-heartedly for a few moments. 'The slide was always my favourite,' he said.

'Go on then.' Pearl pointed. 'It's right there.'

'All right then, I will.' He jumped off the swing and ran over to the ladder. 'I haven't done this for years.'

Pearl dragged her feet on the ground to stop the swing, only remembering afterwards that she was wearing her smart shoes. As Bailey got to the top of the slide, she spotted a multicoloured roundabout. 'I'm so going on that!'

'Here we go!' Bailey pushed off, slid a metre down the chute and then stopped. 'What the—? I'm stuck! This stupid slide isn't wide enough!'

Pearl burst into laughter. 'It's made for five-year-olds.'

Bailey wriggled his way down the rest of the slide, complaining. Pearl, still giggling, gave the roundabout a shove and climbed on.

Bailey rubbed his bottom, smiling. 'You like all the rides that make your head go funny,' he pointed out.

Pearl leaned back and looked up at the sky. 'I guess it's a bit like swimming. You know, when you get water in your ears and the world goes weird. Look!' She pointed. 'The stars are coming out.'

Bailey climbed on next to her. 'If I'm sick, it's your fault,' he warned her.

For a few minutes they spun gently, staring upwards.

'What a mad few months,' said Bailey softly. 'It feels like years ago that I was interviewing you for the magazine.'

'I know what you mean.' Pearl breathed in. 'Then my mum going out with your dad – and my dad turning up again . . . and Harrison's exams . . .'

'And you winning an Olympic medal,' Bailey reminded her.

'Oh yeah, that too.' She smiled.

Bailey sat up. 'I've never kissed an Olympic medallist before,' he said. 'Wonder if it's different to kissing normal people?'

Pearl gazed at him indignantly. 'I *am* normal people.'

He shook his head. 'No, you're not.' He leaned closer. 'You're extraordinary . . .'

And then he kissed her. It was hesitant at first, but when she didn't pull away, he reached out to put his arms around her.

Pearl felt her head spin, and she wasn't sure if it was the roundabout or the kiss. And then she gave up trying to work it out, because something new swept over her. A feeling she knew – a feeling she'd had before – a momentous, stupendous feeling of joy . . .

Just like the feeling she'd had at the end of the Olympics, when everything seemed so overwhelmingly perfect, and she thought she'd never feel like that again.

Pearl smiled as she kissed Bailey back, and the roundabout kept on gently spinning and spinning until she couldn't be sure of anything except the feeling in her heart.

You can meet some of the Sweet Hearts
girls again in the fantastic book

MODEL BEHAVIOUR

Read on to find out who . . .

Chapter 1

such an opportunity!

'I can't *wait*,' exclaimed Lola, stepping into the crystal-clear water and letting herself sink gradually into its warmth. 'Do you think they'd let me design something? I've got this idea for a new bag, you see . . .'

'You don't know which department you'll be working in, though,' her best friend Naiha pointed out. 'You might be put in something really boring, like Pattern Cutting.'

Lola floated on her back and looked up at her friend. They were both tall and slim and beautiful, but Lola was all English Rose with her pale skin and long blonde hair, whereas Naiha's Indian heritage gave her skin the colour of chocolate milkshake and hair as glossy and black as treacle. 'I wouldn't mind. Pattern cutting is really important. But I hope Marisa lets me work in Design.'

'It's lucky your mum is friends with her. I mean,

work experience at Mulberry is, like, really hard to get.' Naiha kicked off her flip-flops and dropped her towel onto a bench. She was wearing a bright yellow bikini, in contrast to Lola's red gingham swimming costume. 'I hope the water is warmer today.'

'It is.' Lola grinned. 'I shivered so much after our last swim, Corin thought I'd caught a chill. He came and turned up the thermostat straight away.' The two girls laughed.

'Your stepdad is a big softy,' said Naiha, stepping carefully into the water. 'He'd buy you the moon if you wanted it.'

'I know. But it's not just me. He's soft with everyone. Mum says it's a wonder that his health clubs haven't all gone bankrupt because he's not tough enough for business.' Lola smiled. 'He's sweet. I can hardly remember what it was like before he came along, to be honest. Louder, I think – and Mum was a bit wilder. But he's a great stepdad, even if he does bang on about having five fruit and vegetables every day. And exercise, of course.'

'You are so lucky to have a pool in your house,' Naiha said enviously. 'I've been trying to tell Mum we need one too, but she just rolls her eyes and comes out with one of her Indian proverbs. "The money you dream about won't pay the bills", or something like that.'

'I thought your dad sent money from India?'

'He does. He's rolling in it! But Mum's always tutting and saying he doesn't give her enough. Do you know how much his last film made? *Millions!*'

Lola swam lazily around in a circle. 'Bet you can't wait to see him next week.'

'I totally can't. It's actually *happening*, Lola. For, like, the first time ever, I'm actually going to see him at work! *And* he says he'll introduce me to Mallika Shan!'

'Who?'

'You know, that amazing Bollywood actress? The one I said was like the Cameron Diaz of the Indian film world?'

'Oh, right. Yeah, I remember.' Lola wasn't entirely sure she did, but she didn't want to upset her friend. Naiha talked about her father's films a lot, and sometimes Lola found it hard to stay interested. 'When did you last see your dad?'

Naiha pulled a face. 'Not for ages. I was supposed to be going out there last summer, but . . .'

'I know.' Lola felt sorry for her. Naiha's dad wasn't the most reliable of people and her friend had been let down badly last year. 'But it's all sorted this time, isn't it? You're really going!'

Naiha grinned. 'Miss Bourne's face when I said I was going to do my work experience in Bollywood! She nearly fell off her chair!'

'I don't think she's used to glamorous stuff,' replied Lola.

'You can tell that by her hairstyle,' said Naiha, rolling her eyes.

'Naiha! Don't be mean!'

'It is awful, though – come on. That thick fringe.' Naiha shuddered.

Lola couldn't help smiling. 'It is a bit dire. I bet Shallika whatshername wouldn't be seen dead with her hair like that.'

'*Mallika Shan*. Honestly, Lola, you're so dippy, you never remember anything.'

'I remember things that are *important*,' said Lola in a teasing voice. Then she giggled, and Naiha did too. 'So, do you think you'll get to be in a scene in your dad's film?'

'That's what I'm hoping,' agreed Naiha. 'I thought I'd just hang around the edges and then, when they're saying, *Oh no, we need another person here, but there isn't anyone . . .* I'd step in and say, "I'm here! I can do it!"'

'That would be the most amazing thing ever.' Lola's eyes shone. 'I'd love to be in a film.'

'Me too.' Naiha sighed.

Both girls silently contemplated their reflections in the shiny ceiling. The pool room was large, with a pair of white pillars at one end. Several reclining pool chairs took up the space along one wall, and two changing rooms and a sauna occupied the other end. Naiha sighed again.

'If I could get on a model agency's books, it would be a great way into films. Can't you talk to your people again?'

Lola pulled a face. 'I did try, Naiha. It's not my fault they said no.'

'I know.'

'Besides,' added Lola kindly, 'it's not as if I do much modelling work myself yet.'

'Not as much as meee!' came a voice from the steps leading up to the kitchen, and Sienna Cassidy, Lola's younger sister, came bouncing down. 'Did I tell you I'm going to do another H&M shoot?'

Lola felt hurt. 'Why didn't they ask me?' The two girls had signed with the same agency three years ago. It had seemed a natural thing to do, following in their mother's footsteps, and it was good fun, trying on the clothes and posing for the camera. But recently, Sienna had been called for more jobs than Lola, and it was beginning to rankle.

'You're too old.' Sienna stuck out her tongue. 'They were looking for twelve-year-olds.'

'Oh.'

'H&M is all right,' said Naiha. 'They've got some good stuff.'

'Yeah, it's cool!' Sienna beamed. Like Lola, she had straight blonde hair and long legs. 'And last time they let me keep some of the clothes.' She jerked a thumb towards the stairs. 'Corin's out this evening and Mum says she can't be bothered to cook, so we're having Thai takeaway.'

Lola cheered up. 'Brilliant. Can we have some of that raita bread?'

'I expect so. Mum's just bunged in the same order as we had last time, I think. She's still working on the launch. Says the caterers are charging far too much and she's mad at Cleo for hiring them.'

Lola and Sienna's mother, Helena Cassidy, had been a successful model in the 80s and since then had dabbled in almost every area in the fashion world, from shoes to bags, make-up to accessories. Her latest project was 'Helena's Whisper', a new perfume to add to her range which already included 'Helena's Blush' and 'Helena's Kiss'. The perfume was due to be launched in six weeks at a swanky hotel, and Helena was spending hours every day on the phone or computer in her study, alternately cajoling and threatening her personal assistant.

'I'm coming in,' Sienna announced, before disappearing into a cubicle and emerging seconds later clad in a sky-blue tankini with silver sequins on the straps.

'That's mine!' exclaimed Lola.

'Not any more,' Sienna told her. 'It fits me perfectly.'

Lola frowned at her sister. 'You should have asked.'

'What for? *You* didn't ask when you borrowed my straighteners yesterday.'

'What have you got planned for next week?' asked Naiha hastily, anxious to ward off a sisterly argument.

'Shopping, mostly.' Sienna shrugged. 'Meeting up with my friends. Watching loads of TV and going to Pret.'

'Boring,' commented Lola, though secretly she was jealous of her sister's plans for half term. It sounded like the sort of thing she'd have liked to do herself, if she hadn't been going to work at such a prestigious design house. She felt her stomach flutter with excitement again. *Mulberry!* It was such an opportunity!

Have you read all the **Sweet Hearts** books?
Discover the entire series

www.ilovesweethearts.co.uk

STAR CROSSED

Fliss isn't exactly outgoing. But on stage
she really comes alive. And this summer,
she's playing Juliet opposite her dream
Romeo – Tom Mayerling.
If only she could tell him how she feels!

But someone else has her eyes on
Fliss's role – and her leading man . . .

ISBN 978 1 849 41205 6

Take a sneak peek at Fliss's diary at
www.ilovesweethearts.co.uk/fliss

STRICTLY FRIENDS?

Megan has had to move two hundred miles away from her home, her dancing and her best friend and ballroom partner, Jake. She's fed up with having to fit in with what everyone else wants.

Then she meets Danny. He's exciting and rebellious and he likes her too. But could there be more to Danny than meets the eye?

ISBN 978 1 849 41206 3

Take a sneak peek at Megan's diary at
www.ilovesweethearts.co.uk/megan

FORGET ME NOT

Kate Morrell used to have it all – fun, friends
and family. But since her mum died three years
ago, Kate can't remember what it's like to feel
properly happy any more.

A summer job at the local garden centre
gives Kate a chance to re-discover the spark
she once had – and arguing with her arrogant
(but gorgeous) co-worker Simon makes her
really come out of her shell!

ISBN 978 1 849 41217 9

Take a sneak peek at Kate's diary at
www.ilovesweethearts.co.uk/kate

ICE DREAMS

Ice skating is Tania's life – she's a champion
in the making. But things have started
to go wrong and she can't tell anyone why
she's become scared of the ice.

When her coach tells her she's got to pair up
with daredevil Zac, Tania is furious. Rebel meets
ice queen – watch out, the sparks will fly!

ISBN 978 1 849 41216 2

Take a sneak peek at Tania's diary at
www.ilovesweethearts.co.uk/tania

MODEL BEHAVIOUR

Lola Cassidy has it all. Model looks,
fabulous friends – life is perfect . . .
Until she finds herself Ugg-deep in mud
at the local animal sanctuary, that is.

But will the week show Lola that there's
more to life than handbags and highlights?

ISBN: 978 1 849 41218 6

Take a sneak peek at Lola's diary at
www.ilovesweethearts.co.uk/lola

sweet
hearts

Go to

www.ilovesweethearts.co.uk

for the latest Sweet Hearts gossip
and goodies, and to find out more
about the author, characters and
other books in this fantastic series.

Each Sweet Hearts book also has a
secret bonus page on the website . . .

For Deep Water, you can take an
exclusive peek in Pearl's secret diary at:

www.ilovesweethearts.co.uk/pearl